Dear C

A very happy 8th birthday from Mr Collingwood and the gang.

We hope you enjoy our story.

Russ x

COLLINGWOOD'S
AMAZING
WILDLIFE
EMPORIUM

Published in the United Kingdom by:

Blue Falcon Publishing
The Mill, Pury Hill Business Park,
Alderton Road, Towcester
Northamptonshire
NN12 7LS
Email: books@bluefalconpublishing.co.uk
Web: www.bluefalconpublishing.co.uk

Cover design by Stephanie Jayne.

A CIP record of this book is available from the British Library.

First printed June 2021

ISBN 978-1912765317

To mum and dad for the bedtime stories

&

To Millie and Finn for the bedtime stories
still to come.

Russell Hurn

Chapter
1

The gentlest breeze stirred the leaves into life as sunlight nudged and teased its way through the tall trees. The sleepy morning was about to be rudely awakened. A howling cry of a baboon cracked the air, sending birds flapping frantically from their nests into the blue sky. Kevin stopped in his tracks. The hair on the back of his neck started to rise. He shielded his eyes from the sun's early rays and stared, partly with excitement and partly with fear.

A large, carved, wooden sign stood in front of him. Bright red letters shouted out 'Collingwood's Wildlife Emporium', and a slightly battered arrow pointed down the winding path. Kevin's ears were now on alert. He heard the gravel crunch with each step he took and then there was another strange noise – and there it was again!

Looking around, Kevin noticed a pigeon sitting in the tree. This one seemed different, though. For a start it was rather plump, unlike the ones that ran with bobbing heads between people's feet in the city centre. This pigeon was sticking out is feathery chest almost as though he wanted everyone to notice his small orange beak and white collar of feathers around its neck. Kevin smiled, thinking of the funny ruffs people wore when Elizabeth I was Queen of England. There was something else, though. The noise, it seemed really strange. As he listened it seemed as if the pigeon, in its gentle coo-coo voice, was saying, 'You're so silly, you're so, sooo silly.' As soon as the pigeon finished another one started up and said the same thing back: 'No, you're so silly, you're so, sooo silly'. Pigeons having a row, how strange, he thought. For Kevin though the strangeness hadn't even begun.

'Ere! We're not open for another half an hour. You'll have to wait.'

Kevin's eyes darted from the pigeon to the large iron gates in front of him, then to a less impressive wooden hut. There stood a rather crotchety-looking man with grey hair and what Kevin thought was a rather comical moustache, although the man didn't look like he was someone who was used to being funny.

Kevin walked cautiously forward and announced in his best grown-up voice, like the one Mum uses when she speaks to her boss on the telephone.

'I've come to see Mr. Collingwood.'

The gatekeeper seemed a little taken aback by the confidence of the young man before him.

'Mr. Collingwood is a very busy man. He don't have time for seeing kids who are skiving off school,' he replied, gruffly.

'I am not skiving, it's the holidays,' Kevin said, enthusiastically, until the gatekeeper managed to deflate his mood.

'Holidays? Oh that's all I need. Hundreds of young yobbos running round trying to sneak in half price, feeding the pigeons ice-cream and taking the mickey out of my moustache. I'm not putting up with it. You tell those friends of yours no one gets in without an adult. I am a black belt in Karachi and I won't take any nonsense this year. I've specially trained a vicious guard dog to help me patrol the area. You tell them.'

Almost on cue, a little brown and white Jack Russell Terrier popped its head out from behind the gatekeeper's legs. Its eyes were wide with excitement, its pink tongue lolling about, and it was panting as if ready to play. Around his neck was a thick studded collar and large bone shaped name tag which read Brutus. Unperturbed by the appearance of his sidekick, the gatekeeper ordered Kevin, rather impolitely, to 'clear off' before turning his back on him.

'But I have an appointment to see Mr. Collingwood about a summer job.'

'I can't imagine why he needs you,' the gatekeeper started to laugh, 'unless of course he's running low on fresh meat for the lions.'

The gatekeeper carried on laughing, obviously very impressed by his own whimsical comments. He picked up the phone and dialled. Kevin had never seen a phone like that before. It was huge. There was a sort of handle that the gatekeeper put to his ear and then a box with a circular dial that moved backwards and forwards making a strange clicking sound. It looked like something Doctor Who would have in his Tardis; well, at least the old Doctor Who that Mum and Dad kept going on about.

'Hello, Susy. How's your dear mother? Really? Give her my fondest regards, won't you?'

As the gatekeeper spoke on the telephone, Kevin gazed through the big black iron bars of the gate, half expecting to see crocodiles snapping their jaws or lions licking their lips and eyeing him up expectantly.

'Oh yes, now, I rang about a boy. There's one here at the gate.' He put his hand over the phone and turned to Kevin: ''Ere, what did you say your name was?'

'I didn't,' Kevin replied, thinking he was being helpful. The gatekeeper gave him a glare that would melt snow.

'Oh, sorry, my name is Doolittle, Kevin Doolittle.'

'And you've come here looking for work with a name like that? Ha, fat chance.' He returned to his phone conversation.

'Hello, Susy, sorry for the delay. This kid reckons his name is Kevin...' he began to smirk and he continued,

'Doolittle. Yes, I know... He's after a job... yeah, reckons he's got an appointment with Mr. Collingwood. I said that Mr...'

He stopped speaking and his bemused expression changed.

'Oh, he has? Well I... I... I thought I had better check. You can never be too sure, can you? Let one of these little beggars in and before you know it they've made off with a hippo. I'll send him over.'

The gatekeeper returned the funny handle to the box with a frustrated crunch.

'OK, you're in, but I've got my eyes on you.'

He put two fingers towards his eyes and then pointed at Kevin, and just for effect repeated the move.

'Turn right at the parrots, turn left at the macaws and the office is just opposite the penguins.'

With that he flicked a switch on the barrier and pulled down a blind on the tiny hut window, saying, 'Closed – back in 5 mins.'

Kevin took his first tentative steps into the park. Noticing there were no crocodiles or lions about to treat themselves to a Kevin breakfast, he walked quickly towards a large cage where he saw four beautiful birds. He looked at them perched on old tree branches that crisscrossed the cage. Bits of fruit and nuts seemed to be scattered on the floor.

Without thinking he said. 'Morning, parrots.'

'Morning, awk.'

Kevin was a little surprised, but had seen enough pirate movies to know parrots could learn to talk.

'Morning,' he said.

'Morning,' came the reply.

Remembering the instructions he had been given, Kevin turned to his right and walked towards another cage of colourful birds. A sign above the aviary said 'Birds of Paradise, Macaws.' Feeling polite, Kevin thought maybe he should say good morning to them as well.

'Morning.'

'Morning' came the response, in a similar scratchy voice.

Delighted, Kevin turned to his left and walked further into the park towards a concrete oval-shaped pool of water. As he approached, he saw another sign: 'Penguin Pool.' Kevin noticed the little black and white birds nuzzling into each other, squawking loudly. One waddled comically to the water and then dived in. The little bird seemed to transform into a rocket beneath the surface.

Kevin had always loved penguins and had watched lots of You Tube videos about them. He noticed there were three different kinds, rockhoppers, with their big feathery ears, Humboldt penguins, and Emperor penguins with their amazing yellow flashes. As he looked around the enclosure, he noticed one Humboldt penguin staring straight at him inquisitively. Kevin turned to go.

'Don't we get a hello, then?' squawked a little voice.

Kevin stopped: 'Wait, what?'

There had been no one near him. He looked around slowly until a large smiley face seemed to blot out the sun and the faint smell of deodorant, only just managing to keep sweaty armpits at bay, began to fill Kevin's nostrils.

'Hi! You must be Kevin.'

In front of him stood a tall, genial man dressed as colourfully as a parrot's plumage. He wore red trousers, a green shirt and a waistcoat covered in pictures of animals. Standing back and raising himself to his full height, he offered a large hand to Kevin, who seemed a little unsure of what to do. Luckily good manners kicked in and Kevin shook the hand, although his face still showed his confusion and uncertainty. This man definitely did not have the squawky voice he had just heard, it was deep and friendly.

'I see you've met some of my lovely birds. Were you talking to them?'

Kevin wasn't sure how to answer but didn't really get the chance.

'You know, sometimes I think they can understand everything we say. Pity we can't understand them, eh? My name is Thaddeus P. Collingwood.'

His deep brown eyes looked directly at Kevin and he beamed an incredible smile, showing off some rather crooked teeth.

'It's a pleasure to meet me, I know.'

Kevin's confusion slowly receded as he figured out this was the Mr. Collingwood of Collingwood's Amazing Wildlife Emporium. The 'Amazing', although not an official name, was the one used in all the adverts that Kevin saw on the posters around town. This was the man he was supposed to be meeting and trying to impress with his love and knowledge of animals and his many personal qualities. There was a list of these, if he could only remember them. Dad had specifically gone through them with him the night before. Reliable and responsible were two of them, he was sure, and maybe sensible was on the list somewhere, but he was less sure of that one.

Mr. Collingwood put his arm on Kevin's shoulder and turned him back towards the penguins.

'They are my favourites,' he said, pointing towards the little black and white birds who were all now diving, with delight, into their personal lagoon.

'That's why I have my office right there,' he continued, pointing to a rickety wood door with 'Private' carved into a rustic piece of bark. 'From there I can watch them all day. What a delight! They do make me laugh. Now, come on, let's have a cup of tea and we can talk about giving you a job.'

With that Kevin was whisked into the little office. Inside it was eerily dark. There were tanks all along one wall. Small lights illuminated bits of twig, leaves and bark, but as far as Kevin could see there were no animals. Mr. Collingwood directed Kevin to an old chair that looked as though mice had been nesting in it and busied himself with a strange silver contraption, which he proudly announced was the 'Collingwood 5000 automatic tea dispensing and brewing system' and 'the only one in the world'. The machine clinked, clanked and clunked into action and shuddered with such a force Kevin thought his tea would be dispensed into his lap rather than into the delicate teacups that had been placed beside it.

'So, Kevin, why do you want to work for me?' Mr. Collingwood demanded, suddenly seeming a little scarier than he had done before. Kevin tried desperately to remember the things he had practised saying to Dad. He had never had a job interview before, and words were jumping and bouncing around his head without organising themselves into any particular order.

'I, uh, I, uh...'

Mr. Collingwood smiled encouragingly.

'I, uh, um...' Kevin's brain gave up trying to be clever and settled for what seemed to be the most obvious thing in the world to say: 'I like animals.'

Mr. Collingwood gazed at him for a while. Kevin was desperately thinking what a stupid thing it was to have said. Why couldn't he have come up with a more grown-up answer like, career prospects or the desire to contribute towards the preservation of endangered species? It was no good though. His brain was now stuck on one thing, the words of those pigeons outside the gates. 'You're so silly, so sooo silly.' The insult in his head was getting louder and louder.

'Ha! Perfect, my boy. What else is there? I think we are going to get on splendidly. Can you start tomorrow?'

Chapter
2

At number 35 Silver Street Lane, Mrs. Marjorie Doolittle was busy being busy. It was something she was incredibly good at. Not a moment in the day seemed to go by without her being on a mission to clean, wash, tidy, fetch, carry or organise. In the midst of her activity, trying to empty the hoover and shoo the cat out the door at the same time, she hollered up the stairs.

'Kevin, come on. It's time you were up. You're late for your lesson.'

No sooner had she encouraged the cat out with a little nudge and shut the door than the phone rang. Mrs. Doolittle didn't like the phone. You never knew who it would be and it always seemed to ring when she was in the middle of a very important job. After all, Hoovers didn't empty themselves, despite the family thinking they did.

She picked up the phone, still holding the Hoover in the other hand, and announced rather quickly, 'Five, one, eight, seven, double two.'

She paused for a moment then switched to her posh telephone voice, which she always liked to use for work in case her boss called.

'Miss Dalrymple, how lovely to... yes, I know I am very sorry, Kevin is a bit late... I do so understand... Yes, we are leaving right away... Of course, I do understand. Goodbye.'

She put the phone down and her pleasant telephone voice with it, before hollering up the stairs in an even more frantic way than before.

'Kevin! Kevin, where are you? We have to leave; you are late. I hope you are not in your room playing on that blessed phone of yours. You know that makes me so cross, when you just let time slip away playing stupid games and watching You Tubey, or whatever it's called.'

With that she pushed open Kevin's door and saw the piles of clothes on the floor. In addition, there were sixteen cups lined up on the windowsill that should have been in the dishwasher days ago. But worst of all, the bed, the bedroom, the cupboard, the toilet, the rest of the house was missing one important thing: Kevin.

Chapter
3

'Over here!' Kevin cried, waving his arms frantically, as if bringing a plane in to park near the terminal.

'Ah good, you got a table, that's great. Here you are, one Collingwood Fruit Fancy and a nice cup of Earl Grey tea for me. Sorry again about the Collingwood 5000. It doesn't normally do that. I am sure the stain will come out.'

He sat down at the table and continued to prepare his cup of tea, dunking his tea bag in and out of the pot, letting it rest each time on the back of the spoon before he dunked it again. After a few minutes and what appeared to be careful consideration of the colour, he went to pour a cup. Unfortunately, the lid wasn't shut properly and the tea ran everywhere except into the cup.

'Oh blast, that always happens.'

With that, his mobile phone rang. Kevin expected Mr. Collingwood to snatch up his phone in an instant and to jump up and stroll around forcefully barking orders and commands like he imagined a businessman would do. Instead Mr. Collingwood sat still, entirely focused on trying to get tea from the pot into the cup and not on to his trousers.

'Aren't you going to answer your phone?'

'Phone?'

'Yes, it's ringing,' insisted Kevin, somewhat unsure whether he should be mentioning it or not.

'Oh, well done, my boy. Can you deal with it, please? It's in my coat pocket.'

Mr. Collingwood was still focusing on saving his trousers from the dribbling teapot as Kevin put his hand in the coat pocket and pulled out a rather out-of-date phone with what looked like an old boiled sweet stuck to the back. He touched the answer button and put the call on speaker, placing the phone on the table.

'Hello.'

A voice crackled distantly on the phone.

'Hello, it's Tom.'

'What?'

'Tom.'

Mr. Collingwood looked confused and bent his head down to the phone. This movement meant the dribbling spout on the teapot edged itself closer to the phone. It was like a brown laser beam from an old James Bond movie, slowly working its way towards the special agent.

'No, sorry, Tom's not here.'

Mr. Collingwood indicated to Kevin to end the call, rolling his eyes and with them the teapot, which continued to pour its liquid contents nearer to the phone. Kevin dived in quickly, just removing the phone in time before tea flooded the table.

'Oh sh- sugar!' Mr. Collingwood cried politely, and he made a grab for a handful of paper napkins to mop up the tea, creating a mini mountain of sodden brown paper that he pushed to the middle of the table.

The phone rang again.

'Shall I?' Kevin enquired and Mr. Collingwood nodded, as he started to remove the foil lid from a little milk pot.

'Mr. Collingwood, it's Tom here.'

He pulled the lid, while at the same time squeezing the little pot. The result was a milk volcano and another mess on the table.

'Oh hello, Tom. Funny, someone called asking for you just a second ago.'

'That was me. I was... never mind. Colly, someone has over fed the sea lions again. They had five buckets of fish instead of four.'

In the meantime, Kevin had opened another milk pot and put it in Mr. Collingwood's tea and was gesturing to see if he wanted sugar.

'Five!' Mr. Collingwood said, nodding.

Kevin was a little taken back. Wasn't sugar supposed to be bad for you? He went ahead dropping five sugar cubes into the cup, each making a satisfying plop.

The voice on the phone continued.

'Can I go ahead and order some more fish, rather than waiting until tomorrow?'

'Yes, I suppose you must. You had better tell Shanice.'

'Just one other thing. Our new addition is taking his first steps. I thought you would like to come and see.'

At that Mr. Collingwood broke into a big beaming smile.

'I'll be right over.'

He stabbed at his phone with his finger, trying to end the call, and muttered something about all adults having fat fingers. He took a sip of his tea, and quickly spat it back into the cup. Recovering quickly and putting a smile back on his face he turned to Kevin.

'So, Kevin, why do you like animals?'

'Well, Mr. Collingwood, I...'

'Call me Colly,' Mr. Collingwood interrupted, 'everyone does, apart from old Harry the gatekeeper. I think he seems to hold me responsible for the time one of the elephants had diarrhoea and...' He paused for a moment and seemed to be remembering something. A smile creeped across his face. 'Anyway, that's another story. Do you have any pets at home?'

'No, Mr..., I, ah, mean Colly. Mum's allergic to everything that's got fur,' Kevin said with a sigh.

'What about having a reptile? A snake would be nice.'

'She's afraid of snakes,' Kevin shrugged.

'What about a goldfish, then?'

'She says they make her feel seasick.'

Colly stroked his chin and winked.

'There's not a lot of hope for your mum, is there?'

He stopped to take another large gulp of the over-sweet tea and swallowed in the most animated way, like a python finishing a rather large meal.

'Right, no slacking, my lad. This park is only where it is today thanks to the dedication and hard work of all its staff.'

Mr. Collingwood waved his arms around to exaggerate the important message he was giving and in doing so knocked a tray from the hands of an unsuspecting visitor.

'Oh sorry, my dear, allow me,' he said bending down to pick up a dusty croissant. As he was stooping forward for the pastry he noticed a dangerous-looking banana skin on the floor.

'Can't have that littering the path, it's dangerous,' he muttered, crawling towards the rubbish. Relieved with the thought he had saved the day, he stood up right underneath another visitor and his tray. There was a thud, a gasp and a clattering as everything went flying. There was a pause and then a swishy flopping sound. Kevin saw Mr. Collingwood in a heap on the floor, covered in raspberry ice-cream, with a cone jauntily perched on his head. Kevin was wishing he'd filmed that for Instagram, because that would certainly have got him more followers. Quickly, he rushed over to offer his hand to pull Colly up.

'Thank you, my boy. What was I saying?'

'You were talking about how hard everyone works here,' Kevin reminded him.

'Yes, there always seems to be something to do.'

As he spoke there was a bustle of activity behind him, with waiters and cleaning staff tidying up the mess and trying to appease everyone. With one eye on the mess and another on Mr. Collingwood, Kevin thought he should try and bring the conversation back to the job.

'Um, you said something about maybe starting tomorrow.'

'Yes, I did, didn't I, that's right. Well, how about we try you out for a week and see what happens?'

'Great!' Kevin beamed. 'That's amazing.'

'Amazing, yes. I love that word. It sounds almost magical.'

Mr. Collingwood looked at his watch.

'Now I must dash. Have a wander around for a while; I am sure the animals would love to meet you. See you tomorrow morning.'

'Bye!' Kevin called after him, as Colly strode casually through the mess of tea, scones, ice-cream and stunned visitors.

Chapter
4

Back at Silver Street Lane Mrs. Doolittle stood at the top of the stairs outside Kevin's bedroom. Her eyebrows were knitted into a tight frown as she tried to figure out what was happening. It was the weekend and a normal Saturday morning would be spent trying to rouse Kevin from his bed, tempting him with bacon sarnies and making threats of removing his games console, but he was always there.

She looked back into Kevin's room, which was festooned with posters of animals, plants and stuffed toys. It looked like a tropical rainforest. Her mind quickly jumped to the first thought that came along. She clasped her hands to her mouth, as she imagined Kevin being kidnapped by a troop of gorillas and was helplessly hanging from a tree, being force-fed bananas.

Mrs. Doolittle's mind flicked to shopping; she must get some more fruit and some apples for a nice crumble for tomorrow's Sunday roast. Her parents were coming and there was always a high expectation for a fruity pudding. Just then, the large grandfather clock chimed 10 o'clock, meaning it was actually about 5 to 10. Why the clock was always five minutes fast she never knew, but it did at least stop her thinking and brought her back to the problem at hand.

Kevin was missing, and it just might be gorillas who were to blame.

Chapter 5

Oogh, oogh, oogh! Kevin waved his arms around mimicking the big, black and rather scary-looking gorillas as he passed by their enclosure. They ignored him. He wasn't the first human who thought they were funny when they did bad impressions of them.

Kevin stopped in front of a small pack of hyenas. He peered into the cage and read aloud the sign that was next to him 'Hyenas - related to the dog family, sometimes referred to as laughing because of their distinctive howling.' He looked at the animals inquisitively.

'You don't look anything like the gatekeeper's trained guard dog,' he said, pulling a funny face at them.

At this, the hyenas began their distinctive laughing howl, which seemed to start as a chuckle and ended up like big belly laugh.

'Oh, you think that's funny do you? Wait until I tell you the joke about the horse, the zebra and...'

'Talking to yourself! You know what they say about

that.'

Kevin spun around quickly. In front of him was a girl. She was pretty and about his age. She didn't, however, look particularly friendly and at the sound of her voice the hyenas backed further away from the fence, becoming uncharacteristically subdued. Kevin felt himself blushing.

'I wasn't talking to myself, I was....'

'Well, I can't see anyone else, only those dumb animals.'

At that the hyenas made a sort of snort sound, turned and walked off.

'What makes you think they are dumb?' Kevin asked.

'Simple! Animals can't talk. They haven't got the cerebral capacity for conversation.'

'They haven't the what?'

'The cerebral capacity. Their brains are too small.' The girl said, tutting. 'Talking of small brains, who are you?'

Kevin was still worrying too much about blushing in front of a girl to have noticed the insult she had just made.

'Oh, hi. I'm Kevin. I've just got a summer job here. Who are you?'

'Shanice Collingwood.'

She announced her name as if she was in a play and was expecting there to be a round of applause.

'Mr. Collingwood is your dad?'

'Duh! You must be as daft as he is.'

'Oh, he seemed really nice to me,' Kevin replied with the best and friendliest smile he could manage.

'Nope! Nutty as fruit cake, just like those dumb hyenas.'

At that she took a swing at a discarded coke can and kicked it at the cage.

'Your dad says he thinks animals can understand everything we say.'

'That's exactly what I mean. He spends hours talking to them. At Christmas he even sings them carols. He thinks if he could understand them, then he would have a really successful park. No wonder Mum left him.'

She looked down at the ground, disguising a sad expression, before raising her head and smiling in a most unconvincing way.

'What do you do here?' Kevin asked.

'Everything,' she said, indignantly. 'If it wasn't for me there would be no Wildlife Emporium.'

Kevin was surprised. Shanice looked about his age, how could she be in charge?

'Don't you go to school?" he asked.

'I'm home schooled,' she replied, gruffly. 'Someone has to organise things, otherwise we would be in a bigger mess than we already are. I hope Colly didn't plan on paying you. That's all we need, another waste of money.'

Kevin was surprised at Shanice referring to her dad

as Colly but given her rather abrupt manner he didn't dare ask why.

Instead he said, 'I just wanted to work with animals. I hadn't thought about money.'

'Then don't!' Shanice snapped.

She turned and walked off towards the office, leaving Kevin wondering what he might have done wrong.

Chapter 6

'Good day, how are you? Buenos dias. ¿Cómo estás? (bleep)'

Mrs. Doolittle was sat in the lounge listening to a Spanish language CD on an old compact disk player. She cleared her throat and tried her best to repeat the exercise.

'Bueenoos die ash, comoo estars?'

The coach on the CD seemed unperturbed by the poor attempt at the Spanish language and continued with the next phrase.

'Very well and you? Muy bien y tu?' (bleep)

As Mrs. Doolittle was gearing up for another try at the language, the front door opened.

'Kevin, is that you?' she called out.

'No, it's a burglar,' came the reply.

Mrs. Doolittle seemed unworried at the comment she had just heard.

'Where is the toilet? Donde esta el inodoro?'

'El inodoro esta arriba,' Mr. William Doolittle

announced as he entered the room.

'What are you on about?'

'The toilet is upstairs,' he said with a smile.

Mr. Doolittle had one of those round faces that lit up when he laughed. He had a big grin almost from ear to ear and a little beard. Mrs. Doolittle used to joke that they must have put his head on upside down when he was born because the top of his head was completely bald, with a little bit of shaded skin all the way round, which seemed to suggest that was where hair should have been, if only he could grow some.

'How's the Spanish going then, luv? Are you all set for your holiday?'

'Well, I think it's OK, or should I say, bano.'

'You could say that, but that means bathroom. You might be better off with buena.'

'Oh, I don't know. It's all Greek to me.'

'Spanish,' Mr. Doolittle whispered under his breath, and then continued, 'Why are you learning Spanish?'

'You know why. I thought it would be useful for our holiday.'

'It would be if we were going to Spain. We are going to France.'

Mrs. Doolittle looked unimpressed.

'Well it was the only CD left in the library. I don't see what the difference is, anyway. Susan Harrow is very impressed with my linguistic skills. She wants me to address the women's church circle on Tuesday,' she said, with a certain amount of pride and a 'So there' look on her face.

Mr. Doolittle let his enormous grin wrinkle its way across his face.

'You know what you need to learn to speak for that lot?'

'What?' Mrs. Doolittle responded.

'REALLY LOUDLY,' he joked, raising his voice. 'They are all over 80.'

He chuckled to himself and was about to leave the room when his wife stopped him.

'It's all right you being flippant, but we have a problem. Kevin is missing. He's not in his room and he missed his singing lesson this morning. I don't know what he can be up to.'

'Oh, he went then.'

'What?'

'He went for that job interview at Collingwood's. He told you the other day.'

Mrs. Doolittle's face dropped as pictures of furry, slimy and wriggly beasts filled her head. She reached for the back of the chair and sat down. Her face had turned a pale green colour.

Chapter
7

Kevin began peeling back the bright yellow skin of his banana, letting four yellow ribbons trail limply over his fist. He was beginning to think that his job at the Emporium may not last very long, as he wondered how he could have said things differently when he met Shanice. His thoughts were interrupted by two female voices talking behind him. Kevin knew it was wrong to listen to other people's conversations, but he couldn't help it.

'If I eat another banana I think I will explode,' said the first voice, quickly followed by a second.

'It's the ethylene gas they pump into them to make them the right colour when they arrive in the shops.'

Kevin looked quizzically at his banana. How did they get gas in there, he thought, and how does that make it the right colour? The voices continued.

'I swear I'm getting lines round my eyes, too.'

'I know what you mean. My skin is losing its orangey glow. If that's not bad enough, I washed my hair this morning and can't do a thing with it now.'

'I know what you mean. It's the water you know. I blame the hippos. They lounge around in it all day long and don't care what else they do in there. The lake's become a positive sewer.'

Kevin couldn't help it. There was something about the conversation that intrigued him. Slowly, he turned round to try and see who was talking.

'I think we should call a residents' meeting. If Colly doesn't do something about it, then maybe we should.'

'You are so right, my dear. It's about time we took some action.'

Kevin parted the leaves of a bush behind the bench, but instead of seeing two ladies as he had expected, he saw two orangutans eating bananas.

'Look out, dear!'

Kevin froze. There were a lot of ideas whizzing around his head. Some were making him feel scared and some excited.

'Were you talking to me?' he managed to splutter.

'Of course not,' replied one of the orangutans. 'We were just'...

'Priscilla!' snapped the second one. The first orangutan stopped, looked directly at Kevin, back at her banana, then at her friend Myrtle, and finally at Kevin again before waving her arms and saying, unconvincingly, 'Ooo, ooo.'

From the path, all Harry could see was Kevin's

bottom sticking out of a bush. He was not amused, and neither was Brutus. That was not the sort of thing you should see in a wildlife park, boys' backsides poking out of bushes. Harry quickened his pace; he was going to find out what this young troublemaker was up to. Brutus followed quickly behind, his tongue lolling from side to side.

Kevin was still staring at the orangutans. Had he been mistaken? There was no one else around, so it must have been them talking – or was he just hearing things? He thought he should check for sure and plucked up the courage to say something. A simple hello might have been sufficient, but in the excitement Kevin started to gabble.

'Hello. Why won't you talk to me? Shanice says you are all dumb, but I don't think you're stupid.'

'Glad to hear it,' Harry said, clearing his throat with a cough and a splutter.

Kevin pulled back and sat on the bench trying to look composed, although having twigs and leaves sticking out of his hair didn't help much.

'Oh, h-h-hello,' he said, brushing himself down.

Harry looked him up and down, and in a slow deliberate voice, said, 'What are you doing?'

'I was... Well, that is I thought I was... that they were... that is, the orangutans were...'

At this point it probably would have been a good idea for Kevin to stop talking, but even though his brain tried to stop, his mouth just carried on.

'I thought they were talking to me.'

'Oh yes,' Harry said, and for a moment Kevin thought he believed him. Harry's face turned into a scowl. 'Do you think I was born yesterday? Very funny. Orangutans talking to you.'

Seeing his owner so animated, Brutus decided he would add to the discussion with a few yaps. Harry lent forward and with one of his large hairy hands, he grabbed Kevin by the collar and started escorting him to the gate.

'Come on, I knew you were trouble. Out you go.'

'What are you doing?' Kevin protested, his feet struggling to touch the ground as Harry whisked him away.

'I'm throwing you out, and don't think of coming back.'

'But I've got a job, I start tomorrow.'

'Oh, ah, and my name's Harry Kane.' The gatekeeper said sarcastically.

'It's nice to meet you, Mr. Kane, but honestly, I've got a job. Ask Colly.'

As he said this Mr. Collingwood appeared, bounding towards them like an excited wallaby.

'Ah, Harry, I see you've met our new recruit.'

'Told you,' Kevin said, pulling himself free from Harry's grip and nearly tripping over Brutus, who was still yapping around his feet.

'Yes, Mr. Collingwood, sir. We were just getting to know each other.'

Harry sent Kevin a look that said, 'Don't you dare say anything or else.' Colly seemed completely unaware that anything else could have been happening and trotted on, contentedly.

'Good, good. Well, I'll see you tomorrow, Kevin.'

Harry's face turned into another rather menacing scowl, different from the one before, but equally as menacing.

'You may have been saved this time, kid, but I'll be watching you. Any funny business and you'll be out those gates quicker than Usain Bolt on a Bullet Train. Understand?'

'Sure,' Kevin replied with a smile, cheekily adding, 'and you have a nice day, too.'

He marched off out of the gate through a large group of head-bobbing pigeons. As they took to the air, Kevin couldn't help himself.

'While you are up there, could you use that guy as target practice?'

Kevin skipped through the gate just in time to jump straight on to a bus heading his way. He settled into a seat and as he looked back, he giggled as he saw Harry waving his fist in the air as a dozen pigeons dive bombed him with their squidgy, white droppings.

Chapter 8

'Here's your tea,' Mrs. Doolittle announced, pushing a large brown mug towards her husband. 'And no dunking the biscuits. You always manage to make a mess.'

She looked up as she heard the front door open, then close, and the noise of someone running quickly up the stairs. Mrs. Doolittle was overwhelmed with a sense of relief and anger at the same time.

'Kevin, is that you? Get down here, your father wants a word with you.'

Mr. Doolittle looked somewhat bemused

'I do?'

'Yes, you do! He disappeared this morning and missed his singing lesson. Miss Dalrimple was quite distressed.'

'I don't know why you keep on at him about those lessons. H hates them and to be honest he's hopeless.'

Mrs. Doolittle looked horrified.

'Sh, he might hear you. Anyway, that's not the point.

It is an art. He needs to be musical if he is to become friendly with Charlotte.'

Mr. Doolittle rolled his eyes.

'What? Susan Harrow's daughter? She's a conceited snob just like her mother. There's no way she's likely to become Kevin's friend or anything else you may have your mind set on.'

Mrs. Doolittle was just working herself up to the point of giving her husband a good tongue lashing about the importance of social etiquette for eligible young bachelors, and the delights of mixing with the right type of people, if he was ever going to amount to anything in this world, when Kevin sheepishly entered the kitchen.

'Hi.'

'And just where have you been all morning? You missed your singing lesson. I had Miss Dalrimple on the phone wondering where you were. She was all of a dither, which is not good for a woman of her age. And as for your father he was worried sick, weren't you, William?'

'I was?' He noted the glare from his wife and changed the tone of his answer quickly. 'I was!'

Kevin moved to the cupboard and began searching for snacks. He caught his dad's eye, who gave him a discreet wink.

'I told you I don't want singing lessons anymore. I hate them.'

Mrs. Doolittle was shocked. In fact, her eyebrows moved so high up her forehead they disappeared beneath her wavy ginger hair.

'Well, what else are you planning to do with the next six weeks? I'm not letting you lounge around the house watching You Tubey videos or making those funny noises on that computer of yours.'

Mr. Doolittle decided it was probably the right time for him to get involved in the conversation. He could see emotions starting to boil and had a distinct feeling he would probably end up getting the blame if things carried on the way they were going.

'Mum was wondering where you were, sunshine.'

'I told you yesterday; I had an interview for a summer job at Collingwood's Wildlife Emporium.'

Kevin had said this with a certain amount of pride and was hoping for a positive reaction. His mum's face fell.

'Collingwood's? How could you do that? All those furry, slimy, smelly animals. Ugh! I think I'm going to be sick.'

'How did you get on, son?'

'Great,' Kevin beamed. 'I start tomorrow.'

Dad was clearly pleased and got up to give his son a man hug. This basically involved a loose hug with some pats on the back and some animal-like grunts.

'Well, that's wonderful. Well done, son!'

'And what about his singing lesson?'

Mrs. Doolittle was not letting this lie and had begun to waggle her finger around, indicating how serious she thought the situation was.

'Mum!'

'He'll still have to practise. Miss Dalrimple has entered him into her Songs from the Shows Extravaganza on the 20th. Here you go, you can start practising.'

She produced some sheet music with a flourish and handed it to Kevin, before he sloped off upstairs.

'One day, when that boy's Prime Minister, he'll thank me for making him take singing lessons.'

Mr. Doolittle managed to hold back a little smile as he buried his head back in the local newspaper. Upstairs, Kevin began to sing. The tune was unrecognisable and for some reason all Mr. Doolittle could think about was yesterday's TV documentary on howler monkeys in the forests of Brazil.

Chapter 9

An elephant trumpeted its alarm call as the rays of the early morning sun crept into Kevin's room. It wasn't the trumpet of a wild African elephant gracefully marching across the savanna, but a mechanical squeak of his alarm clock buzzing into life at 7 o'clock.

Kevin woke. There was a second or so as his brain booted up and realised what day it was, then a massive surge of energy as he realised it was his first day at work. He rushed out of bed and down the hall towards the bathroom. He was just about to pass his parent's room when the door opened and his mum, struggling with her sleep mask, staggered in front of him and slid sideways into the bathroom and locked the door. With a huff, Kevin trudged back to his room and collapsed on the bed for a snooze.

An elephant trumpeted again, and the clock clicked to 10 past 7. Kevin was awake again and on route to the bathroom when his dad emerged from his room, yawning and scratching his way to the bathroom, closing the door in his son's face. Kevin added a puff to his usual huff and headed back to his room. He fiddled with his clock then flopped on to his bed for another snooze.

For the third time the elephant sounded. Kevin rubbed his eyes and rolled over to turn off the clock, which now showed 8 am. With an 'Argh' he raced for the bathroom. He is almost there when a giant white rabbit wearing a yellow and blue bow tie jumped out in front of him and into the bathroom. Kevin screamed. His screams echoed around the landing and were mixed with the elephant trumpeting. He felt his feet rising from the floor as a big grey trunk wrapped around him and lifted him up and on to the elephant's back. He could feel the animal's rough grey skin and thick hairs as the mighty beast started walking down the stairs towards the front door. Kevin held his breath as they broke down the door and most of the porch before emerging into the bright sunlight. Kevin closed his eyes. The trumpeting was getting louder and louder. Kevin opened his eyes. He was in his room and the alarm clock was blaring. In a daze he looked at the time; it was 8 am. Kevin rushed out of bed and then hesitated. He had a strange feeling a white rabbit was about to appear.

Downstairs, Mr. and Mrs. Doolittle were discussing the merits of Nutty Granola versus Special K as the radio busied itself with an old tinkly tune. Mrs.

Doolittle allowed herself a little hum to the tune, then got a bit self-conscious and went back to her cereal.

There was a gallomping on the stairs as Kevin hurriedly descended.

'He's not going out without breakfast, is he?'

Kevin popped his head around the door.

'Bye, Mum. Bye, Dad.'

Mrs. Doolittle gave him her 'What do you think you are doing?' look and added, 'If you'd got up earlier you wouldn't be in such a rush. Now, I've made you bacon and eggs. You need a good breakfast.'

'Thanks, Mum,' Kevin replied, 'but I'll just take some fruit.'

'There's some nice bananas on the sideboard,' Mr. Doolittle announced as he pushed his Nutty Granola to one side and helped himself to the bacon and eggs.

'No thanks, Dad. All that ethylene gas makes them taste so artificial these days.'

His parents exchanged a look of confusion.

'Where did you hear that?'

'Just a conversation I overheard yesterday.'

Mrs. Doolittle wriggled on her chair and was obviously feeling uncomfortable with the way the conversation was going.

'Kevin, you shouldn't listen to other people's conversations. No good ever comes of it, you mark my words. Now, more importantly, what about your singing lessons?'

'Sorry, Mum, I gotta go.'

Mr. Doolittle managed a smile as he shovelled in the salty bacon and warm eggs. He watched his son grab an apple and head for the door. Mrs. Doolittle did not seem quite so content with the situation.

'Kevin, don't go bringing any of those dirty animals home with you. I've just had the carpets cleaned and Susan Harrow is coming this evening on committee business.'

'No, Mum,' were Kevin's final words as he shut the door and ran off towards the bus stop.

Mr. Doolittle was enjoying his bonus meal so much that he had taken to buttering some bread and was now running it around the eggy mess on the plate, much to the disgust of his wife.

'I'm not sure this job will be safe, William. He could be attacked or, worse still, catch some horrible tropical disease.'

'He'll be fine, luv.'

'I'm sure Miss Dalrimple would not take kindly to teaching someone with a tropical disease. And I would appreciate it if you could check his pockets for small furry things every night, just in case something...' Mrs. Doolittle shuddered at the thought, 'in case something tries to use him to make an escape.'

Chapter 10

Kevin jumped excitedly from the number 44 bus and wearing his most innocent and charming smile ran up to Harry.

'Hello.'

'Hm, you're back, are you? Well remember, no funny business. I'll be watching you.'

Kevin bent down to stroke Brutus, who backed away slightly.

'Brutus is a vicious guard dog, I shouldn't get too close if I were you.'

On cue, Brutus dropped to the ground and rolled over, exposing his white fluffy tummy as an invitation for a tickle. Kevin readily stroked the little dog's belly and then behind his ear. Brutus was obviously enjoying the attention and his little pink tongue started lolling from side to side and little bits of drool ran down his cheeks.

Harry was not amused by the behaviour of his assistant and made a half-hearted excuse.

'Lucky for you he is on his tea break at the moment.'

Kevin stood up and headed to Mr. Collingwood's office. Brutus was still lying on the floor expecting more strokes. All he got was a nudge from Harry's size 10 boot, spurring him back on to his feet with an excited, 'Yap! Yap!'

As he entered the main building, Kevin could see a younger man waiting with Colly. He was dressed in green work clothes with the Collingwood's Wildlife Emporium logo embroidered on to his shirt and underneath, the name Tom. He had strong hands, a stubbly chin and wavy hair. He was looking seriously at his boss while he was finishing a telephone call.

'Well, I think it might be a rather good idea if you found it. After all a 7-foot python attacking OAPs is not going to be very good publicity for us, is it?'

He cleared his throat and slammed the phone down as if emphasising his leadership on the matter. Unfortunately, the force on the phone hitting the table was enough to knock the nearby teacup on to its side and its earth-like brown contents started to meander across the table, seeking out bits of important paperwork to deposit their markings on.

With perfect teamwork, Tom righted the cup and began dabbing frantically with a cloth, while Colly scrabbled with the papers trying to get them into some order, occasionally shaking them dry in the process.

Kevin tentatively knocked and opened the door.

'Is it OK to come in?'

'Yes, of course, my boy. Come in, come in. Welcome to Collingwood's. This is Tom, our Head Keeper. He'll show you the ropes.'

He paused, just long enough for a little old lady to come bustling into the now cramped office.

'Ah, here is the lovely Mrs. Ainsley, our beloved tea lady. How long is it you've been working here, Mrs. Ainsley, 30, 40, 50 years? I think it's so long even the elephants have forgotten when you arrived.' He laughed joyously at his own wit.

Mrs. Ainsley looked like a delightful character, sort of a jolly grandmother who probably made amazing cakes and could beat anyone in the family at Scrabble.

'I was here with your grandfather Cecil Collingwood, sir, as you rightly know, so none of your cheek. You're still not too big to go across my knee for a good hiding.'

Kevin wasn't sure whether that kind of threat would be at all realistic, because he was pretty sure Mrs. Ainsley would break if Colly lay across her knees, but the thought of the boss getting a slapped bottom from this little old lady amused him. Mrs. Ainsley popped a fresh cup of tea on the desk and cleared away the old cup, muttering something under her breath about the mess of the office and what would his grandfather think.

'She never forgets to remind me how she used to bounce me upon her knee, Tom. She'd be hard pressed now though,' Mr. Collingwood said, patting his portly belly. He sat back in his chair laughing and tried to put his feet up in a cool relaxed way. It wasn't to be. He caught the lace of his tatty desert boots on the corner of the desk, causing him to tip backwards on his chair, kicking the table and sending the new teacup into a shuddering frenzy in the saucer. Tom was quick to react, but too far away to be helpful. Kevin watched as the latest cup of tea jumped from the saucer and with amazing accuracy deposited its entire steaming contents down Mr. Collingwood's front, provoking an understandable yelp of pain.

'Ah, Mrs. Ainsley I... I seem to have spilt my tea.'

'There's a surprise,' she muttered. 'You'll find your spare shirt in your top drawer, where it usually is.'

'Actually, I had to use that one earlier. I got into a bit of a mess when I was watering the bonsai.'

Mrs. Ainsley gave him one of those looks that mums everywhere seem to develop when they have a two-year-old child in the house.

'I'll bring you another one when I've taken the scones out of the oven.'

Mr. Collingwood gently pulled the soggy remains of his shirt away from his belly where it had been sticking and in an effort to get himself into action he slapped his hand down hard on the table with a purposeful, 'Right, to work.'

Kevin wished he had been filming the next bit for

his You Tube channel, because Mr. Collingwood's hand caught the bowl of the teaspoon that had fallen from the saucer. It flew through the air and neatly into a waiting cup on Mrs. Ainsley's tea trolley.

'Thank you, dear,' she announced, as she pushed the little trolley out of the door and down the corridor.

There was a moment of calm in which no one really knew what to say. Colly finally broke the silence.

'Well, Tom, what about showing Kevin our latest addition. I'm sure you could do with some help there.'

'Good idea, Colly.'

It was the first time Kevin had heard Tom speak and he detected a smooth accent, which he thought might be Irish or Scottish. Together they left the office and walked out into the park. Just as they passed Colly's window they heard a crash, a shout and some language that Kevin thought would definitely not be on his mum's list of acceptable words and phrases to be used in polite society.

Chapter
11

Kevin and Tom made their way around the park to a large enclosure. As Tom unlocked the keeper's entrance, Kevin waited excitedly, trying to imagine what the latest edition to Collingwood's could be; possibly some equipment or a new way of doing things or... Before he could get to a conclusion, he saw Harry walking past. He appeared to be talking into a small voice recorder.

'09.15 hours. Kevin Doolittle seen at giraffe enclosure. All quiet for now.'

He then turned his attention to his little dog trotting merrily along beside him.

'Keep your eyes peeled, Brutus. I have a feeling today is going to be eventful.'

With that, he made a gesture towards Kevin, pointing two fingers at his own eyes and then turning them to point to Kevin.

'I'll be watching you,' he mouthed.

Tom then popped out from behind a green

camouflaged door and beckoned Kevin towards him.

'I am going in to feed them and see if our newcomer is up to seeing visitors. In the meantime, you can do a spot of tidying up. There's lots of rubbish around here. It's not a glamorous job, but essential for animal safety.'

With that, he handed Kevin a black plastic bag and some rubbish pickers. They reminded Kevin of the toy T-Rex head and jaws he had as a kid. You squeezed the trigger, and the mouth would open and close. He remembered with a smile trying to pinch Dad's ears when he was snoozing.

'There's a bin over there. I'll be back in ten minutes,' Tom said, before disappearing back behind the door. Meanwhile, Harry had moved a few metres away.

'09.20. Suspect is left alone with company equipment.'

He pulled Brutus' lead and together they hid behind a tree as Kevin began his litter picking duties. Kevin had just deposited two coke cans, a water bottle and a Mars wrapper in the bag when a young voice behind him made him jump.

'Helloo.'

Kevin looked carefully around for the owner of the voice, half expecting to see an orangutan. He was alone. Only a baby giraffe stood unsteadily just inside the enclosure, his long neck waving slightly as though he was unsure how to control it.

'Helloo.'

Kevin, blinked, shook his head and rubbed his eyes. The voice he could hear quite clearly seemed to be coming from the giraffe he was staring at. He shook his head again, trying to knock any silly ideas out of his brain, then continued his work.

'I'm a giraffe. What are you?'

Kevin's surprise was now turning to annoyance.

'OK, who's playing the trick? Very funny, ha-ha, a talking giraffe.'

From behind his tree, Harry was intently studying Kevin's movements and recording his comments.

'09.22. The boy is behaving suspiciously and now seems to be talking to himself. What do you think, Brutus?'

On hearing his name the little dog yapped enthusiastically, then returned to the pleasure of scratching his ear with his back foot.

'My name's Jeffrey. What's yours?'

Kevin was now feeling a bit nervous. There was no one around and yet he clearly heard a voice talking to him and it seemed to be coming from the young giraffe behind him.

'You can't be talking to me, you're a giraffe.'

Kevin wasn't expecting a response; rather, he thought that someone would jump up from behind a bin or something and start to tease him. But no, the voice continued.

'Yes I am. What are you?'

'I'm Kevin. No... no!'

Kevin's frustration was clearly visible to Harry. From where he was, the gatekeeper was pretty sure something odd was going on.

'Stay here, Brutus. This calls for some high-level observation.'

While Brutus switched to scratching behind the other ear, his owner began trying to grab an overhead branch.

'I'll be back in a moment.'

As Harry struggled slowly into the tree he had been hiding behind, Kevin was also struggling to understand what was happening.

'Don't you want to talk to me? Don't you like me? Is it my long neck? I knew someone would think it was funny.'

'No, no I like your long neck, it's just that... Agh, what am I doing? Animals don't talk.'

The little giraffe tilted its head on one side and looked boldly into Kevin's eyes.

'Who says so?'

'Everyone. People talk, animals just make funny noises: snort, barks, growls, that sort of thing.'

By now Harry had managed to get his legs around one of the branches and was holding on like a snoozing sloth.

'All animals talk, but not all Kevins listen.'

'What does that mean?'

'I think it means some Kevin's only hear what they want to hear.'

While the unusual conversation was continuing, Harry was determined to get close enough to hear what Kevin was apparently saying to himself. Unfortunately, his plan involved edging slowly along the branch he was on, whilst recording everything he saw.

'09.28. Suspect seems to be talking to...'

Harry paused for a moment thinking. He realised he was enjoying this. He had always wanted to be a detective and had spent many years as a youngster watching TV cops do battle with villains of all shapes and sizes and he always imagined himself in a fast car, lights and sirens blazing, rushing around the city catching bad guys. He was so involved in his thoughts he didn't hear the crack. He did hear a bark from below.

'Quiet, Brutus, this is a covert operation. Discretion is the name of the g-a-a-a-me!'

His last words were heard reverberating around the park as the bough of the tree broke, throwing Harry to the ground with a thump. Kevin looked round, but failed to see Harry, who was lying in a heap under the tree. Luckily, Brutus was on hand to offer some medical assistance and set to work on licking Harry's ear.

Kevin turned back to the enclosure at the sound of a gentle female voice.

'Jeffrey, it's lunch time. Where are you?'

The little giraffe in front of him turned his long neck

right round to look towards the sheds in the enclosure.

'I've got to go. Bye,' he said, before trotting off on his wobbly long legs.

Kevin uttered a similar 'Bye,' but was really in too much of a daze to know exactly what was happening.

'Did you see our new recruit then?' Tom shouted as he came out of the keeper's door. 'I was sure he came out here.'

'Huh?'

'Young Jeffrey, the baby giraffe. Did you see him?'

With these words Kevin was shaken from his daze.

'Ah! Yes, yes, I did.'

'Well, what do you think?'

This was one heck of a question for Kevin, because he was thinking so much at that moment. His brain was buzzing like a beehive.

'I think he... he was amazing.'

'Yep, we're very proud of him and his mother adores him.'

'She said that?' Kevin queried, without really thinking.

Tom laughed jovially.

'If only she could. That would be a story for the papers. Finish up here and I'll show you around the rest of the park.'

Chapter
12

Back in his office, Colly was again on the phone, but this conversation was very different from the one about the escaped snake. Mrs. Ainsley was sitting in a chair nearby, knitting a bright blue scarf.

'7.30, that will be fine, and don't forget the pink carnation. Until then, goodbye.'

Mr. Collingwood made some strange slurpy, kissy-kissy noises into the phone before hanging up. Mrs. Ainsley gave him a rather queer look.

'Don't you think you should tell Shanice?'

Mr. Collingwood seemed surprised and just slightly embarrassed at the idea his tea lady had just suggested.

'Oh, Shanice won't mind.'

'All the same, I think you should tell her. She is your daughter.'

At that moment Shanice burst into the office carrying a pile of paperwork.

'Tell me what?'

'Ah,' her father said looking down suspiciously at his

lap.

'Nothing, dear, just some ideas I have for the future.'

He sat back in his chair, sipping a cup of tea.

'Humph! Well, there won't be a future the way you are going. You have to save money. Look at this bill.'

'It looks much like all the others to me, dear.'

'Two hundred pounds for tea?' Shanice's tone was cutting, and her eyes drilled directly into her father.

'Is it really? I never realised I drank that much tea.'

'You don't,' she snapped. 'It usually ends up down your shirt. Look, here's a £300 bill from the dry cleaners.'

The shock of the amount of the bill caused Colly to cough and splutter on his tea spilling it down another clean shirt.

He quickly jumped up shouting, 'Agh. That's hot.'

Then he noticed the fish tank. He delved his hand into the lukewarm water and started splashing on his chest. Realising what it was he was doing, he suddenly became very apologetic.

'Sorry about that,' he said to the fish, before turning back to his daughter. Shanice just glared at him with utter teenage disgust.

'Colly! You are hopeless,' she snorted and stormed out of the office.

Mrs. Ainsley had been quietly knitting the whole time and without looking up just commented, 'What that girl needs is a mother figure.'

'I know. I'm working on it,' Colly replied, as he continued to wipe the remnants of the tea from his shirt.

Mrs. Ainsley smiled sweetly to herself.

'Heaven help the poor woman,' she said.

Chapter 13

In the giraffe enclosure things seemed more tense than usual. The female giraffe had bent her long, slender neck almost in two to look directly into the eyes of her young calf.

'Now tell me the truth, Jeffrey. Were you talking to the human boy?'

'Human? He said he was a Kevin.'

'That is his name, Jeffrey, but he is a human like the keepers. Were you talking to him?'

Jeffrey's big brown eyes looked up at his mother, his bottom lip curling over into an almost comical sad face.

'Yes, Mama.'

His mother rose to her full 5 metres in height and glared down at him beneath her long eyelashes.

'How many times have I told you not to talk to strangers?'

She didn't stop for an answer and her tone of voice seemed to just get harsher.

'And especially, never...' She paused for effect, moving her head closer and looking straight into his watering eyes: 'Never talk to humans.'

'But Mama, he seemed very nice.'

'Humans can't be trusted; they don't care about us.'

'But Mama,' Jeffrey insisted.

'No buts, you are not to do it again.'

His mum then bent down, her neck nuzzling against her son. Her voice had calmed, and she spoke gently but directly to him.

'Do you understand, Jeffrey?'

The little giraffe nodded, and his big shining eyes started to swell as a small pool of tears gathered in his eye lid ready to spill on to his brown and white cheek.

'Yes, Mama.'

Chapter 14

Two more coke cans, half a hot dog and an endless number of Maoam wrappers: Kevin was beginning to think that the people who visited the Emporium were probably the messiest people on Earth. The BBC could make a whole documentary on the rubbish he was collecting. He imagined himself addressing a TV camera as the host of his very own show, Doolittle's Great Discoveries.

'Here at Collingwood's Wildlife Emporium we can see the extent of the problem. Human beings have discarded their waste of all shapes and sizes, and this threatens the safety of the wildlife, like these hyenas here.'

He looked into the enclosure at three hyenas who were slumped together in a heap.

'Enjoying your new job?' came a voice to his side.

Without thinking, he replied, 'Let me guess, you're a talking hyena.'

'Do you mind!' snapped Shanice, walking quickly

towards him as if she were ready for a fight.

'Oh sorry, um, yeah, it's OK, I guess. I didn't really know what to expect.'

'Most work experience kids we get here expect to be lion taming. Hah! Losers.'

'Shanice, you know everything about the park, right?

'Yep,' she replied quickly.

'Do you know if anyone has, um, has anyone noticed anything unusual about that baby giraffe?'

'What do you mean?'

'Well, you know, anything unusual!'

Kevin jerked his head towards the giraffes, trying to emphasise the 'unusual' part of the question so Shanice would understand.

'Anything unusual, that is, for a dumb, ruminating, quadruped with a 3-foot-long neck, spots and horns? Nope, I don't think so.'

'No, I mean...' Kevin paused trying to think: what did he mean?

'I mean, anything different.'

'Well, there is just one thing.'

Kevin was suddenly excited.

'What?'

'Well in a certain light, he's a dead ringer for Prince Harry.'

'Very funny.'

Kevin was beginning to think this conversation was hopeless, but he was determined to try again.

'I mean, have you spoken to him?'

'Yes, I guess you could say that,' Shanice replied.

Kevin looked shocked, but inside felt like fireworks were exploding in his tummy. Shanice had talked to the giraffe; he wasn't imagining things this was really happening and it was amazing.

'What happened?' he managed to blurt out.

'It was when he'd just been born and he was having difficulty standing up. I asked him if he was drunk.'

'And what did he say?' Kevin's excitement was now near to bubbling over.

'He said he had a slight problem balancing, but he would soon get the hang of it.'

'Really?'

'No, of course not, you idiot.'

Kevin felt his excitement instantly turn to embarrassment and his body highlighted how he was feeling by making his cheeks go bright red.

'Colly really got a bum deal when he hired you,' Shanice scoffed.

In the background the hyenas began their annoying laugh. Shanice gave them a withering look and they skulked away.

'I've got more important things to do than talk to a nerd like you.'

And with that she stomped off, leaving Kevin feeling rather stupid. As he looked at the litter around him Kevin heard the woodpigeons calling again. '

You're so silly, so sooo silly.'

He felt a surge of embarrassment and anger building in his tummy. Noticing another discarded coke can, he swung a kick with all his strength, sending the can flying across the path and clinking noisily against the fence.

Chapter
15

Howls, growls, barks and squawks filled the air as Harry and Mr. Collingwood surveyed the park. Harry was nursing his left arm, which was now in a sling after his fall, while Mr. Collingwood stood starring out across the various enclosures as the sun started to send long shadows towards him.

'I don't know what to make of it, Mr. Collingwood. I haven't heard such a din since the karaoke at last year's staff Christmas party.'

'The animals certainly seem agitated. I hope Tom's not been doing his Ed Sheeran impression again,' quipped Mr Collingwood.

Kevin was feeling a bit weary. His first day had been much harder work than he'd imagined. Apart from the litter picking, he had also helped with mucking out, fence repairs and feeding. Although he had thoroughly enjoyed his time, he was glad he was leaving for home. He weakly waved as he passed Harry and Colly at the gate.

'See you tomorrow.'

'How did you get on today, Kevin?' Mr. Collingwood replied enthusiastically, although his attention did seem elsewhere.

'It was... very interesting, Mr.... I mean Colly.'

'Well, if you have any questions give me a call. I'm always keen to talk about my animals.'

'I'll remember that, thanks. What did you do to your arm, Harry?'

The gatekeeper was not happy that Kevin had asked, and a flash of anger and embarrassment crossed his face,

'It was Brutus. He got a little bit excited chasing away some villain.'

Brutus looked up at his owner. With big round, 'Tickle my tummy' eyes, he rested one of his paws on Harry's big black boot.

Kevin didn't believe Harry's story one bit, but he was too tired to try to find out any more right now.

'Oh, OK. Bye, then.'

Harry waited for Kevin to get out of earshot before deciding to share his concerns about the new employee.

'About that boy, sir.'

'Yes, Harry. Nice lad, isn't he. Anyway, must dash.'

Harry begrudgingly agreed with a false smile and a grunt.

'I suppose you're off home as well then, sir.'

With that, Mr. Collingwood's eyes lit up with a certain excitement.

'No, not tonight, Harry. I have a date.'

'A date, sir?'

'Yes, a delicious creature, short, dark and loves fish.'

Harry instantly imagined Mr. Collingwood in a restaurant chatting to a penguin.

'This is someone very special, Harry, so mum's the word. I'll leave you to lock up. Goodnight.'

'Of course, Goodnight, sir.'

Harry shut the gate after his boss and then stared back into the park where the noise was growing into cacophony. Brutus was now looking worried. He sat at Harry's feet. His tail and ears were down, and his head was drooping. The little dog had a sense that something was about to happen that would affect them all. Harry seemed to notice it, too, and bent down to give the little pooch an affectionate stroke.

'Are those beasts getting to you, Brutus? Me too. It's a good job we're not on the night shift; this place is beginning to give me the heebie-jeebies.'

Chapter
16

Silver Street Lane was again basked in the yellow glow of the early summer evening. The smell of chips wafted down the road from the mobile chippy van that parked on the green every week. At number 35, the odour of steak and onions was still hanging around the kitchen and Mrs. Doolittle was trying to shoo it out like a cat into the garden, partly to get the smell out, but also partly to let the neighbours know how posh they were having steak midweek. With one hand she waved the newspaper around like a giant fan while she strained to see the time on the kitchen clock. It was a quirky Swiss cuckoo clock that she had bought many years ago when she had gone skiing with Mr. Doolittle, for their honeymoon. It had one of those annoying ticks that was punctuated on the hour by a plastic bird popping out from behind a little door with a rather piercing 'Uck-oo' sound.

'Oh gosh, where is Susan? We will be late for Step class.'

Mrs. Doolittle was wearing her workout gear. It comprised multicoloured tights and a leotard with some rather thick leg warmers. Mr. Doolittle used to tease his wife about her 1980s gear and even offered to take her shopping for something more modern, but Mrs. Doolittle had worn the same outfit for 30 years and had no intention of changing now – unless Susan did, of course.'

'Did you finish the crossword, luv?'

'Almost, there is one I missed, I think.'

'Do you think I could have a look before you accidently send it flying into the garden?'

Mrs. Doolittle handled him the now rather tatty newspaper as she paced up and down looking at the clock.

'Ah here it is. Three down. "This ruminating animal would need a high collar." Seven letters, the last one is an E.'

'Giraffe,' Kevin said as he strolled into the kitchen.

'What?'

'Giraffe. That's a ruminating animal and it would definitely need a high collar, probably one a couple of metres high.'

'Well done, my boy,' his dad said, as he searched the kitchen for a pencil or a pen or anything to complete the puzzle.

'Where are all the pens? Why can I never find a pen when I need one? Honestly we get through more pens than toilet tissue. What is going on?'

'There's one behind your ear, Dad.'

Mr. Doolittle looked a little bit embarrassed as he slumped back into his seat.

'Helping on the crossword, huh? That job seems to be rubbing off on you.'

'Yes, I had an interesting conversation with a...'

Kevin stopped mid-sentence. He was desperate to say what had happened, but was convinced he would only be laughed at, even by Dad, who tended to believe everything Kevin told him.

'I hope you haven't had anything rubbed off on you. All those animals with their disgusting habits and fleas.' Mrs. Doolittle eyed her son suspiciously. 'I suggest you get those clothes off and put them in the washing machine right now!'

'Who were you chatting with, son?' Mr. Doolittle enquired, having put the paper away. He was aware he probably should be doing a job like taking the bins out but fancied chatting to his son a whole lot more.

'Oh no one really. Well, it was just a, umm, a... girl.'

'A girl!'

Those two little words suddenly sparked his mum's interest as she started putting on her rubber gloves, so she could peel Kevin's contaminated clothes from him.

'And who might that be?'

'It's Colly... I mean Mr. Collingwood's daughter, Shanice.'

Mrs. Doolittle stared down her nose at her son as she removed his jacket. She held it at arm's length and, using as few fingers as possible, she tried to manipulate it into the washing machine.

Mr. Doolittle was smiling.

'A job and a girlfriend all in one day. No wonder he doesn't want singing lessons.'

'Dad, she's not my girlfriend, she just works there. In fact, I don't think she likes me very much.'

Mrs. Doolittle turned around with a look of horror and disbelief on her face.

'Nonsense. What girl could resist this lovable little face?'

She grabbed her son and squeezed his cheeks, finally planting a huge kiss on his forehead and leaving a large lipstick mark.

'Mum!' Kevin pushed her away, trying to wipe his head with his sleeve.

At that point the doorbell rang. Mrs. Doolittle stood to attention, rather like a meerkat looking out for danger.

'That'll be Susan. I'm off. See you later. And William, do make sure Kevin gets those clothes in the washing machine as soon as possible.'

With that, she left in a swirl of green and yellow Lycra, greeting Mrs. Harrow at the door with, 'Susan, darling, how lovely to see you.'

Chapter
17

On the other side of town, Collingwood's Wildlife Emporium was noisier than the northern runway at Heathrow Airport. The animal cries had continued since Kevin left and just seemed to get louder and louder.

In the lion enclosure, a mature male sat motionless with his eyes closed. Within an instant his manner changed, as he opened his eyes and held back his head, releasing a mighty roar.

The lion turned to address a gathering of animals who had managed to escape their enclosures to stand before him.

'Silence!'

Albert had a deep majestic voice full of authority and wisdom.

'Silence!' he repeated over the park's residents' excited chatter. To ensure everyone heard, there was a well-orchestrated system of yelps, hisses and growls that relayed messages to all the animals, even the meerkats at the back, who stood in a row on their hind legs, looking fearful. After a few seconds the noise stopped, until a single hiccup from one of the seals sent a Mexican wave of sniggers around the audience.

The lion cleared his throat and addressed the crowd in the same way a judge might talk to his court.

'It has been brought to my attention that there has been a breach in secrecy and that someone...' he paused, looking slowly around the assembled audience, '... someone has spoken to a human.'

There was a commotion in the crowd and Jeffrey, the young giraffe, was pushed forward to stand alone in front of the formidable beast. Jeffrey hung his head in shame. His heart was beating loudly in his chest and he could feel his tummy tighten into a hundred knots.

The lion looked directly at the little giraffe, then snorted through his nose. He raised his head high again.

'I am not here to apportion blame for this irresponsible act; that will be dealt with personally.'

Jeffrey felt the weight of those words pushing down on his shoulders. He knew he was in trouble and so did everyone else.

The lion continued, 'However, I would just like to stress to everyone the importance of not communicating with humans. We all know they are dangerous and unpredictable creatures. I trust I will not have to make any further comments on this matter.'

He waited as the yelps, hisses and growls carried his words to the back of the crowd.

'Now, is there any other business?'

Priscilla, the elderly baboon Kevin had seen eating a banana, tentatively raised her hand, wiggling her long slender fingers as if she was shouting 'Cooee' to her friends.

'Excuse me, your honour, I would like to make a comment.'

Albert the lion sat back on his haunches.

'The floor is yours, Priscilla.'

'Thank you, your honour, sir. I was just going to say that as far as humans go, I like them.'

'So do I, but I couldn't eat a whole one,' squawked Conan, the vulture, flexing his talons. This comment caused the hyenas to break into a combined cackle.

Amongst the laughter, three little Humboldt penguins pushed their way to the front of the crowd, ducking in between the other animals' legs.

'We like the humans, too,' announced Flo, Mo and Bo in perfect harmony.

From the hippo pond came a large splash and a rather unpleasant grunt.

'That's hardly surprising, is it?' scoffed Howard, a rather large and formidable male hippo.

He raised his massive body from the lake, shaking muddy water from his back and turning a group of beautiful pink flamingos into a rather soggy mess, so much so that they looked more like large dirty dish mops sticking out of a washing up bowl.

'You have always been the humans' favourite. That cutesy image makes me sick.'

Ignoring the bickering that seemed to have started, Albert turned his attention back to the baboon.

'Priscilla, it is a well-known and accepted fact that humans are untrustworthy.'

'And stupid,' chipped in Chester, the chimp, picking his nose and dangling upside down from an overhanging branch.

'Not all of them,' smiled Myrtle the orangutan, looking wistfully into the distance. 'What about Sir David Attenborough?'

At the mention of David Attenborough's name there was a general increase in twitters, grunts and snorts as the animals all started to speak.

'My auntie in Morocco met him once,' said Stulla, a rather elegant stork, flapping her wings as if trying to get everyone to notice her.

Albert's patience was growing thin. Whilst he did agree that David Attenborough was an exception to the rule, he feared the animals were getting rather distracted from the task in hand.

'Please can we get back to your point, Priscilla?'

'Let me see.' She paused and let her eyes drift upward as she scratched her chin. 'I said I liked the humans, didn't I?'

A number of the other animals started to move about uncomfortably, expecting this may be a rather long thought process.

'But there was something else.' Priscilla could feel the glare of the other animals on her as she struggled to remember.

'Oh yes, I know. It concerns the water we are all supposed to be using; it seems to me some animals are not showing due respect to cleanliness.'

'Oh strewth, here we go again. The Duchess is off,' splashed Howard, turning his back and letting himself sink back into the muddy water ,with some rather embarrassing bubbles.

'It may not seem of importance to someone as crude as you, but others amongst us have a certain appearance to uphold.'

'A mud pack is usually good for the appearance,' cackled one of the hyenas.

Feeling flattered that someone was taking her seriously, Priscilla took the bait.

'Do you think it would improve my looks?'

'Yes, until it falls off!'

At that, the hyenas roared with laughter, slapping each other on the back in delight.

'That is just the type of ignorance I am talking about, your honour,' Priscilla continued, unperturbed. 'There is no respect for others these days, I remember when I was younger, there...'

Albert cut in.

'I take your point, Priscilla. Yes, water is important for everyone and I have noticed problems myself. We need a fresh supply of water for each enclosure.'

At this point, Conan the vulture let out a chilling cry of frustration.

'And just how do you propose to organise that, your high and mightiness?'

'At this present time I am not sure Conan, but we will find a way.'

More animals were shuffling from foot to foot now and there was a sense of unease, like children thinking their parents were about to have a row.

'And what about my living conditions?'

The animals' attention turned to Paco, a large polar bear who had raised himself up on to his hind legs and was staring across the group towards Albert.

'You said you would find a way to improve them and stop me pacing up and down all day.'

'I have not forgotten, I was...'

'And what about me?' trumpeted Janet, the Asian elephant

'And me,' came the rumbling growl of Gnasha, the tiger

'And us,' hollered the chimps.

'I am aware of all the problems we face as a community and I ask you again just to be patient.'

The word patient didn't seem to go down well with the animals, who reacted with another cacophony of screeches, growls and grunts.

'I have consulted with the holy tortoise and the sage has foreseen a bright future.'

'We don't need a weather forecast, we need action,' snarled Gnasha, exposing his sparkling sharp teeth.

'Give me a little more time is all I ask and do not try anything rash without my consent,' said Albert.

The general murmurings of discontent continued around the park. Albert felt now was a good time to bring things to a close.

'Now, if there is no other business, I suggest we adjourn this meeting.'

The growls faded into grunts and sniffs of disdain as the animals returned to their enclosures and slowly the park fell quiet again. The only animal stirring was Jeffrey. He was stood outside staring up into the night sky.

'Look, Mum!' he cried. 'A shooting star! That's good luck, isn't it?'

Chapter
18

The town of Honeymarsh was a quaint English market town that bustled with life on market days and on other days was as quiet as a church. Tucked away down a side street was a little restaurant called The Watering Hole.

Colly stood at the bar looking nervous. He was on his third apple juice and thinking of ordering another. On his scarlet jacket he wore a pink carnation. The door opened and he looked expectantly towards it, then sullenly glanced down at his watch letting out a rather large sigh. Turning his attention to the flower on his lapel, he fiddled with the carnation, trying to remove it. He gave off a muffled cry as the pin fixing the decoration pricked his finger. In frustration he yanked at the flower, which came away, along with a slither of material from his jacket that hung down like a leaf in need of watering.

The force of the movement shot his arm backwards, knocking over his drink on the bar. As he moved to catch the glass, he tipped his stool in front of a passing waiter, causing him to trip and catapult his tray of drinks into a customer's lap.

Colly quickly popped the carnation into the rubbish bin by the door as he left the bar, and the mêlée behind him

Chapter 19

Kevin was lain on his bed. In one hand he had an Action Man and in the other a plastic giraffe. These were toys he hadn't looked at for years. He had found them while tidying his cupboard and was using them now to try to understand what had happened earlier. He was going over and over the conversation.

The action man was saying the things he had said, and the giraffe was saying what he had heard. Despite how real it had seemed at the time, the more he went over it now the more he couldn't believe he really had spoken to a young giraffe.

'Hello, my name is Jeffrey.'

'My name is Kevin.'

There was a knock at his door and his mother bustled in fussing around picking up stray pairs of pants and closing his cupboard doors before trying to tuck him into bed.

'Time for sleep, Kevin,' she said as she planted a wet kiss on his forehead.

'Mum?'

'Yes, darling.'

'Do you think animals can talk?'

Kevin could feel nerves rumbling around his tummy as he heard the words leave his mouth.

'Don't be silly, Kevin.'

'But what if they could?'

'You really must control that imagination of yours. Now, go to sleep.'

'Night, Mum.'

In the soft beams of light through his blinds, Kevin looked carefully at the two toys. He shook his head and threw the toys in the general direction of the cupboard.

'I must have been dreaming.'

Chapter 20

Mr. Doolittle sniffed in disgust and slammed the paper down on the table.

'Politicians! They make me so mad!' He grabbed his 'Greatest Dad in the World' sandwich box and headed for the door. 'I'm going to work.'

'Don't forget my sister is coming to stay tonight,' Mrs. Doolittle called after him.

There was a pause and then a bemused head peered back into the kitchen.

'Josie, is coming tonight?'

'Yes, it's on the calendar. She is staying for a few weeks while she sorts out her new house. I told you last week.'

Mr. Doolittle's face seemed to be frozen. His bemused look had changed to shock.

'I...'

'So be nice darling.'

His wife blew him a goodbye kiss and pulled on her rubber gloves to tackle the washing.

As Mr. Doolittle turned, Kevin bundled down the stairs.

'All right, Dad?'

Huh, yeah, it's just... Did you know your Aunt Josie is coming tonight to stay for a few weeks?'

'Oh no, that means lentil burgers for tea.'

They exchanged a look of suffering before laughing.

'Kevin, is that you? Come and have your breakfast.'

Kevin trudged sleepily into the kitchen and popped himself down at the breakfast table, as his mum placed a plate of eggs and some colourful-looking sausages in front of him.

'Mum, are these vegetarian sausages?'

'Yes, darling. Auntie Josie is coming, and I thought we should try them out. That green one is lentil and spinach and the purple one is beetroot and black bean. Bonnie Apetitey.'

Kevin sighed, grabbed the ketchup bottle and covered them all in a thick, red, saucy blanket. Mrs. Doolittle was not amused. Not only did she detest ketchup, because the smell made her feel sick, but she was upset that Kevin didn't appreciate the effort she had put into defrosting and microwaving such a lovely breakfast. To make a point she huffed and puffed about the kitchen for a few minutes.

Kevin didn't notice. He was too busy thinking what the day would bring.

Chapter
21

As Kevin walked through the gates of Collingwood's Wildlife Emporium that morning, the memories of the day before came flooding back. He was so lost in his thoughts he didn't notice the glare from Harry as he walked past Security. He was met at the office by Tom and eagerly offered to help out with the giraffes again. He was rather hoping that it would be an uneventful day, so he could just get his life back to normal and not have to worry if he was hearing things or not.

Kevin busied himself with preparing the hay, carrots and high-fibre biscuits. He helped Tom attach the acacia leaves to the tree trunks in the giraffe enclosure and all the while the little giraffe he had spoken to seemed to be ignoring him. Every time Kevin approached, the little giraffe turned its back and was hurried to the other side of the enclosure by his mother.

'You look a bit distracted, Kevin. Are you all right?'

Tom's smooth Celtic accent took a while to get

through to Kevin's brain, but when it finally realised someone was talking to him he jumped.

'What? Huh, sorry.'

'Are you all right? You look like something is bothering you. Is everything OK?'

'Yes, of course', Kevin snapped back a little abruptly.

He was feeling a little silly and embarrassed that Tom had noticed he was lost in his thoughts.

'Come on, let's finish up here, then I could do with your help with the macaques.'

Kevin picked up his tools and followed Tom out of the enclosure. As he left, he couldn't resist a little look back at Jeffrey, who at that very moment turned towards him. Their eyes met for a second and Kevin felt there was a little smile on the giraffe's face before his mother nudged him away with her long slender neck.

The macaque's enclosure was completely different from the open space the giraffes had. It was like a little jungle with trees and branches tightly packed together. As Tom and Kevin approached, the little monkeys started shrieking and bouncing amongst the branches.

'I think these are one of my favourite animals,' Tom remarked as they got nearer. 'They always seem excited to see me. I guess having a big bucket of fruit might help but I love the way they scamper in the trees, and when they look at you it's like they are thinking up mischievous ways to trick you. One of them stole my baseball cap last week and took it up to the top of the tree where he ....' Tom paused and looked uncertain what to say. 'He um... did a number 2.'

Kevin burst out laughing and his eyes went to Tom's cap on his head.

'Yep, it was pretty disgusting. It's OK, I threw that cap away this is a new one,' Tom added, flipping his cap around back to front.

'Can I hold one?' Kevin said as he got to the cage.

Tom turned to address him squarely.

'I know they look cute, Kevin, but there are a few things you need to remember. Always stay calm and don't look them in the eyes. If they want to come near you they will, but let them decide. These have been raised with humans from birth, but they can find handling very stressful, so we only do that for their medical checks.'

The little monkeys were now scurrying and squeaking excitedly above them.

'Now, they love their fruit and leafy vegetables, but we also give them some insects, nuts and seeds and scatter them around, so they can forage like they would in the wild. They can also catch diseases from humans, so many keepers use face masks. I think it stops us communicating with them, though.'

'Communicating with them?' Kevin's eyes were wide with astonishment at what Tom had just said.

'Yes, there is a lot of communication. Facial

expressions are very important in a macaque colony.'

'Oh, I see,' said Kevin, his excitement suddenly dampened.

Kevin followed Tom's instructions as they placed the food around the enclosure. All the while the little primates scampered overhead. Kevin stood looking at the hustle and bustle above him and noticed that all of the monkeys seemed to be moving back and forth from the far corner. Inquisitively, Kevin stepped over the large tree trunk lying in the cage and moved to the corner. There was one macaque who was lying still on a branch. One of its legs was draped over the side and it seemed to be coughing. Instinctively Kevin spoke as he slowly moved forward.

'Are you OK, little one? You don't look so good.'

The little monkey looked at him with sad eyes. As Kevin gazed compassionately another macaque leapt from the nearby branch on to his shoulder. Kevin froze. He wasn't quite sure what to do now, but standing still seemed to be a good idea. He could feel the little primate's breath on the back of his neck and then he heard it.

'He's not very well, he's got a virus.'

Meanwhile Tom had moved back to the entrance and was picking up the buckets.

'Let's go, Kevin. The penguins won't feed themselves.'

The macaque spoke again. This time it was more of a shriek but the words were clear, at least to Kevin.

'Get him some help,' and with that the monkey sprung back on to the branch.

'Ah, Tom, I think this one has got a virus or something, he's not moving.'

'Ah, he's probably sleeping'

'No, I really think he is ill. Look!'

Tom moved the last remaining buckets into the keepers' area and came towards Kevin. His usual happy-go-lucky face quickly flipped to concern.

'I think you are right, Kevin. Well spotted.'

He grabbed his radio from his belt and after a few crackles spoke quickly into the transmitter.

'Colly, this is Tom. Do you read?'

The radio crackled and hissed for a few seconds.

'Colly, are you there? This is Tom. We have a monkey down, code 911. Over.'

The radio crackled again and then Colly's voice came through.

'Receiving you, Tom. Please confirm where you are, and we will call the vet.'

Tom passed on the details and as he spoke the other monkeys sat still. As they left the cage the noise and scampering started up again. One of the macaques jumped from the tree to the wire mesh.

As Kevin looked back he was sure he heard a little, 'Thank you.'

Chapter
22

The rest of the day was full of hustle and bustle. The vet arrived within the hour and there was a huddle of keepers around the enclosure all trying to see what was happening with the little monkey that looked so frail and vulnerable amongst the crowd. After a while the crowd dispersed, and Tom came to find Kevin.

'Hiya, it's OK, the monkey will be fine. The vet has given him some antibiotics. Things could have been a lot worse if we hadn't noticed he was poorly. You did a good job, mate.'

Kevin beamed; he was enjoying the praise. At the same time, Colly came bounding over, his red flared trousers waggling either side of his spindly legs. Shanice was just behind him studying some paperwork, which looked like more bills.

'Well done, my boy. You've certainly made quite an impression in your first week. I think we will have to keep you on a bit longer, if you're enjoying it here.'

'Oh yes, please, Colly, sir, that would be fantastic!'

'Super. One thing I don't understand, though, is, how did you know the macaque was ill?'

Kevin's smile dropped. What could he say? He certainly had no knowledge about animals and their ailments.

'A little bird told me. Well, actually, a little macaque.'

Colly laughed in a jovial way, patting Kevin on the back.

'Well, maybe I should reward them instead of you,' he said, winking. 'On your way home, pop into the souvenir shop and say I said you could take a little something home.'

Shanice scowled.

'Another waste of money,' she muttered under her breath.

The rest of the day was uneventful. There were no confusing conversations with animals. In fact, most of them seemed to move away when Kevin got anywhere near them. On his way home he did as Colly had suggested and popped into the souvenir shop. The assistant smiled when Kevin mentioned what Colly had said. He wandered around the shelves of stuffed animals, drinking cups with wriggly snake straws and brightly coloured t-shirts with every possible animal imaginable. Kevin finally noticed some rather ugly looking rubber insects and in particular a life-sized rubber tarantula. Well, he thought, Auntie Josie is coming to stay he might just have a bit of fun with something like that.

As he passed the security gate, Kevin noticed Harry adjusting a rather large sling that was around his neck cradling his left arm.

'You OK?' Kevin enquired.

'Oh yes. This? Yes, just a Karachi injury when I was training last night,' Harry replied, making some rather strange swinging motions with his good arm and kicking his leg out to the side, frightening Brutus under the chair.

'I thought you said you and Brutus were chasing a villain.'

Harry looked stumped, then annoyed, then thoughtful.

'Yes. I did, didn't I? I am glad you were paying attention. It was thanks to my amazing skills in Karachi that we were able to apprehend the villain. I only noticed I'd hurt myself when I was training and doing my usual hundred push-ups,' Harry finished, with a rather weak smile.

Kevin now seemed even more confused as to what had happened, but chose to say nothing. Brutus was now sniffing around his feet, so Kevin bent down to give him a little tickle behind his ear before saying goodnight. Brutus yapped a happy reply.

Chapter 23

Kevin was just turning the corner into Silver Street Lane when he noticed a taxi pull up outside of his house. From the back emerged a woman in her forties with bright ginger hair, a teal skirt and emerald green jacket, topped off with a large pair of Dr Martens boots tied up with pink laces. There was certainly no mistaking Auntie Josie. The next moment there was a high-pitched squeal from the house and his mother came running down the path, her arms flapping excitedly. Kevin got to the house just as the hugging and kissing was finishing, but not late enough to avoid them altogether. Josie grabbed him in her bear-like grip, pulling him towards her. Kevin was immersed in the sweet and calming fragrance of Josie's lavender perfume.

'Grab Josie's bags, Kevin, I am sure she is gasping for a peppermint tea.'

Kevin dragged two very heavy cases up the path to the front door. Half tripping, half falling with style, he deposited the luggage and himself into the hall.

On the front of the cases were stickers from the many exotic locations Josie had travelled to: Brazil, Ecuador, Malaysia and one that said Bognor. The rather naughty part of Kevin's mind suddenly whirred into action and he carefully unzipped his auntie's suitcase and pushed his rubber tarantula inside. Then, with a bigger than normal smile, he disappeared upstairs.

Chapter
24

As the sun turned orange and sank behind the western downs, the long shadows of two men followed them past the entrance to Collingwood's Wildlife Emporium. The men and their shadows stopped outside the gate. They could see Harry sipping tea and feeding biscuits to Brutus. One of them took a moment to speak into his phone, then quietly they both moved on past the entrance and disappeared into the dusky darkness.

Chapter
25

Kevin pushed the last remnants of his sweet potato and quinoa veggie burger through the gloopy pile of ketchup. Josie had started on her story of an adventure in the Ecuadorian rainforest. This was the fifth adventure she had recounted and both Kevin and his father rolled their eyes. However, this story just might get a little more interesting. Josie had just sprung up saying she had brought a gift for the family. She went to the hall and dragged her case into the dining room, which had been opened up and thoroughly dusted before the arrival of its special guest.

'So I was deep in the rainforest and the parrots were flying overhead cawing and the rain was trickling down through the leaves and I noticed this.'

At that moment Josie opened her suitcase. There on top of her tie-dyed t-shirts sat the tarantula Kevin had got from the shop. What followed was a scream that would have scared monsters away.

Mrs. Doolittle jumped up on to her chair and

shrieked, 'Kill it! Kill it!'

Auntie Josie seemed a little more relaxed.

'Now everyone, it's OK. It is one of nature's creatures, we cannot kill it. I know what to do; just stay perfectly still.'

Kevin was enjoying this immensely and tried not to smile as he looked from face to face. His dad didn't seem to have noticed the spider and was looking around the room, wondering what had made his wife jump on to her chair.

'Kevin, go and get the broom,' Josie ordered, and Kevin dutifully ambled into the kitchen. He thought he wouldn't rush as this was far too much fun.

When he came back into the dining room his mum was hopping from foot to foot on the chair like she was standing on hot sand at the beach. Josie was staring intently at the suitcase, while his dad seemed to be looking for his glasses.

'Kevin, give the broom to your father.'

'It's OK. I think I can manage,' said Kevin, as he approached the suitcase and the rubber spider, carefully trying to act scared and brave, while desperately wanting to laugh hysterically.

'Hit it! Hit it!' shouted his mum.

Kevin swung the broom down on to the suitcase several times. This seemed to reduce the anxiety in the room considerably, although Josie's face had now turned to horror as she watched the fake murder happening in front of her. Kevin then bent down to pick up the spider prompting another screech from his mum and this time Josie, too.

'It's OK. It's not real. I got it from the Wildlife Emporium,' Kevin announced with a laugh and a waggle of the toy towards them.

Josie and Dad both laughed, adding comments like, 'Oh, you should have seen your face' and 'I've never seen you jump like that.'

Mrs. Doolittle was a little more reserved with her response. She carefully got down off the chair, smoothed out her skirt and announced, 'I think I'll make some tea.'

Chapter
26

It was trying to rain as Kevin entered the park the next day. It was the sort of weather than can't make up its mind if it really is raining or not, and there was just enough breeze to make Kevin shiver as he passed the Security gate. Harry was pacing up and down with a look of deep concentration on his face.

'Are you OK?' Kevin enquired in his friendliest voice.

'Something is up, my lad, mark my words. My bunion has been throbbing all night. There's trouble on the way.'

Kevin smiled in an 'I'm sure everything will be all right really' kind of way and headed for the office.

He could hear excited chatter as he opened the door. Colly was wandering around waving his arms in a rather theatrical manner and seemed very excited about something. Shanice was busy scribbling notes on her pad and Tom was looking thoughtful.

'Ah Kevin, my boy, it's all very exciting isn't it?'

'What is?'

'Tell him, Shanice.'

Shanice lifted her head from her note book and opened her mouth, but Colly's enthusiasm cut her off before she could say anything.

'We have a new guest coming, Kevin, all the way from Russia. She is magnificent and just might be the answer to our problems.'

With that he did another lap of his desk, clapping his hands together in delight.

'What he means is we have been successful in our bid to be part of the Captive Breeding Programme for the Amur leopard. A female from Vladivostok is coming to the park tomorrow.'

'Yes, yes, yes. Isn't it wonderful, Kevin?'

Kevin was sure it was wonderful, although was still trying to understand completely what this meant.

'Tom and the other keepers will be checking everything is OK for the enclosure this morning, Kevin, so you can give him a hand. You will get to meet Fyodor our male Amur leopard; he's in for a surprise I can tell you. Now, where's Mrs. Ainsley? I am in desperate need of a celebratory cup of her finest tea.'

With those words he left the room, his hands still clapping as he hurried towards the kitchens.

'Wow, it sounds amazing,' Kevin declared excitedly, before Shanice offered a more sobering tone.

'It could be, but we have a big responsibility to care for the new leopard and we have to hope she gets on with Fyodor. If they don't hit it off we could be in worse trouble than we are now.'

Shanice swept out of the room in her usual 'I'm too busy to stay and chat' manner.

'You are right, Kevin, it is amazing, but it's going to be hard work. Come on, let's go and see our Russian prince.'

Kevin followed Tom out of the office. He was walking quickly and Kevin was struggling to keep up. The rain was more persistent now and Kevin was glad he had worn his cap and raincoat. Tom, on the other hand, was in his shorts and t-shirt and seemed completely unaware of the weather. They wandered past the coyote enclosure before heading into Big Cat Territory. The lions, tiger and cheetahs were all sheltering from the rain either under trees or in their sleeping quarters. At the end of the run of enclosures, they came to one Kevin hadn't noticed before. It was surrounded by a high black and rather ornamental iron fencing.

'This is the home of Fyodor, our Russian prince. Do you know much about Amur leopards, Kevin?'

Kevin shook his head. He knew what a leopard was, but the way Tom was talking made this one sound rather special.

'Well, you won't see many of these. Since 1996, the Amur leopard has been classified as critically endangered. There was a time when it was estimated that fewer than 70 individuals were thought to exist in the world. Sadly, us humans are to blame. It's hunted and killed for its beautiful fur while its habitat is being destroyed for houses and farming. There are just a few worldwide in captivity, and we have one.'

As Tom finished speaking, Kevin saw the shape of a leopard move from the shadows towards where they stood. Fyodor was magnificent. He moved quietly and stealthily, keeping his eyes locked on to them. As he approached, Kevin could hear his breathing. The animal stopped just in front of them at the fence, starring into Kevin's eyes. It then looked at Tom and moved closer, rubbing his face against the fence.

'Hello, Fyodor, this is Kevin. We've got some news for you buddy. You are going to get a mate.'

The leopard stopped, turned away from them and with a leap disappeared into the trees.

'He's not the friendliest of animals is our Fyodor, so let's hope he can brush up on his social skills before the princess arrives. She will be in the enclosure next to him to start with, so we need to make sure everything is spotless for the new guest. Come on, it's going to be a busy day.'

Tom was right; the day was busy. Kevin soon forgot about the weather as he helped the keepers clean, repair and generally spruce up the empty enclosure next to Fyodor's. By the time he left that night he was ready for his bed. As he walked past the Security gate,

Brutus gave him a friendly goodnight yap; and as Kevin looked over at Harry he could see him sitting in the booth, rubbing his feet and muttering under his breath.

Chapter
27

As the noise of a lawn mower gave way to the melody of the song thrush, the residents of the wildlife park gathered for their weekly meeting. There was even more chatter than the previous meeting and it took a rather large roar from Albert the lion to settle everyone enough to begin.

'There are two main items we need to discuss tonight. The first is the news that Fyodor overheard today. As you may have noticed, the keepers were unusually busy today repairing the enclosure next to Fyodor, who has informed me that we are expecting the arrival of another big cat. I expect everyone to welcome our new resident and make them feel at home. I myself remember the stress of being moved here from Longleat and how hard it is for those first few days.'

He turned his attention to the leopard who was sat to his left.

'Fyodor, as the new resident will be living next to you, could you organise the usual introduction to the park, the rules to living with each other, the health and safety tour and of course the "no eating residents" policy?'

Fyodor shifted uneasily at the responsibility, but nodded in agreement. He hadn't said the new animal was supposed to be his mate. He could imagine the teasing he would get from some of the other animals if they thought he had a girlfriend.

'Maybe we should have a welcoming party,' announced Priscilla, clapping her hands together in delight.

There were some general murmurings of agreement from the other animals, especially the younger ones who loved having an excuse to stay up late.

'Let us wait and see what our new friend would like first, rather than arranging something at this stage.' Albert replied in a rather sensible parental way. 'But yes, it may be a possibility.'

Albert continued to address the other animals with his usual air of superiority.

'The second item we need to discuss was another breach of the 'no talking to humans' rule. This time it was the macaque community.'

At that, all the animals turned towards the little monkeys, who began bowing their heads in embarrassment. One of them, Marvin, who had been the one to whisper in Kevin's ear, started to try to explain, but the glare from the other animals seemed to take away his power of speech and he sat quietly waiting for the telling off that he felt was surely coming his way.

'I have looked into this case,' Albert continued, 'and it seems to me this incident, while in breach of our rules, was, in fact, understandable.'

There were a few gasps from the animals, some from disgust and others astonishment at what their leader had just said.

'The action of one of our junior members, um...' Albert searched his memory for the name of the little monkey, 'Marvin, does seem to have been timely in helping to save the life of his brother.'

There were more gasps now and Marvin felt the knot of fear in his tummy relax. Maybe he wasn't going to be told off after all.

'It does appear that this boy Kevin has a good heart. I am reminded of the story of our ancestors when they first came here. For the younger ones amongst us who have not heard the story, back then there was a special relationship with Master Cecil. He was Mr. Collingwood's grandfather and founder of the park. He, so legend tells us, won the confidence of the animals and used to speak with them regularly. Is that not so, Pollyanna?'

With that he turned to an elderly grey parrot who was perched on a branch beside him. She flapped her wings in acknowledgement and continued the story in a rather squawky voice.

'I remember when we first came here, the animals came from all over the world. Sadly I am the only survivor of that time. It was agreed by the animals back then that, given the harsh and different environment of the park, we would work together and ask Mother Nature for help. We did not expect what happened, but somehow Master Cecil was able to understand our many languages in the same way we do. Some say he is our spirit human, others that he was an animal in a former life; but whatever the reason, the relationship we had enabled us to live good lives and the park was successful. Sadly, the skills Master Cecil had were not passed down to his son, who, as we know, lacked interest in the park. Our current Mr. Collingwood also does not seem to have developed these skills either, although we all know he is clearly dedicated to the park, if rather incompetent in how he runs it.'

'Yes, thank you, Pollyanna,' Albert butted in. 'Bearing this in mind, I am suggesting that in an effort to help improve all our lives in the park that maybe...' The great lion paused and gathered his breath and thoughts.

'That, maybe I should meet with this boy Kevin to see whether he may be able to help us.'

The park was so silent that you could have heard a spine drop from a porcupine's bum.

'What do you think?' Albert looked around taking in the open mouths and blank expressions.

The animals could not believe what they were hearing. Many of the older ones new the legend of Master Cecil, but had never really believed it and therefore had not passed on the story to their young ones.

At that moment, a beam of light swept across the enclosure lighting up Albert's magnificent form. He roared and Harry, who was holding the torch, jumped in fright. He dropped the torch which flickered off. By the time he picked it up and fiddled with the batteries the animals had dispersed. Brutus was yapping excitedly, but Harry could see nothing unusual as he directed the torch's beam around the paths, enclosures and even into the treetops. Everything seemed normal, so why, thought Harry, was his bunion hurting him so much? With a tug on Brutus' lead, the pair continued their night patrol.

Chapter
28

Kevin was up and out of the house in record time the next morning. He had not even bothered to wax his hair, which was a big thing for a teenage boy. Arriving at the park, he saw Harry marching up and down like he was on parade, while behind him the other staff members looked a lot less formal. They were all stood around in little groups chatting and laughing. Kevin had just exchanged a few 'Good mornings' before a large yellow lorry pulled up to the gate. There was a container on the back with some foreign writing on the side. In the cab there was the driver and two other men who were wearing green t-shirts and looked a lot like the keepers at Collingwood's. Harry marched to the gate and saluted as Mr. Collingwood joined him. There was a brief discussion before the driver revved the engine and clunked it into gear. Harry made a great display of pushing the button to raise the gate and then waving the lorry through. There was a round of applause from the staff as the lorry drove past the crowd and followed Tom, who was driving one of the park vehicles.

'Come on, Kevin, you don't want to miss this,' Tom shouted.

Kevin jumped into the back of the Land Rover as the convoy headed towards Big Cat Territory.

Back at the road there was another vehicle. This one stopped opposite the gate. No one got out, but inside two pairs of eyes watched the activity intently.

After what seemed to be an age of manoeuvring, reversing, beeping and revving of engines, the lorry came to a halt. Tom spoke to the keepers and Kevin could detect a strong accent when they spoke, even though their English was excellent. The three worked together to lower the crate slowly to the ground next to the entrance to the enclosure.

They opened the door to reveal the sleeping body of a leopard. One of the foreign keepers, who Kevin figured must be a vet, gave the leopard an injection. They then retreated to a safe distance, ensuring the leopard had a clear path from the cage to the enclosure through a specially built wire tunnel. Slowly the leopard seemed to wake. First her eyes opened, then she raised her head and finally stood, a little shakily at first. She then moved slowly to the door of the crate and sniffed the air before retreating back again. She continued to do this, gradually moving further into the tunnel. Kevin could see her amazing patterned fur and the lightness of the coat compared to pictures of other leopards he had seen. Kevin noticed the new sign that had been erected. It showed a map of Russia and Korea with a red dot indicating where the leopard came from. Underneath was some information about the species. The pale fur apparently helped the Amur leopards to camouflage themselves with their surroundings. Then in big letters along the top of the sign was the name of their new resident, Fefina.

Suddenly the leopard bolted into the enclosure. She stopped on the mound in the centre and looked around. Her eyes took in everything and Kevin had a sense of awe just looking at the animal. He wasn't the only one.

In the enclosure next to them, Fyodor was also watching intently.

Chapter 29

The rest of the day was as busy as the day before. Kevin could only remember sitting down for five minutes, just enough time to wolf down a bacon sarnie. The park was busy, too, not because of visitors, but rather everyone seemed to be in a hurry. In the office the phone was ringing constantly. Shanice had decided to contact the local newspapers and radio station about the new visitor and within hours she was dealing with reporters and producers, who all wanted to interview Colly about the new resident. Harry was in his element at the gate, where he was demanding to see the identification of all the press people who turned up. As Kevin headed wearily for the exit, he heard a 'Psst' noise, coming from one of the large rhododendron bushes in the park.

'Psst.' Kevin edged closer. 'Psst.'

'Hi, is anyone there?' he said, as he pulled back some of the branches.

There amongst the dark green foliage was a meerkat

about 30cm tall, standing on its back legs.

'Aw, hello, you're cute.'

'Cute? Who are you calling cute?' said the meerkat, in a rather rough cockney accent. Kevin had half expected him to sound like the meerkats on the TV adverts for insurance, but this little creature was definitely not one of them.

'Sorry, it's just...'

'I know, you've seen the TV adverts. Well, for your information those are not real meerkats, mate.'

'No, of course not, sorry. Did you want me?' Kevin said apologetically.

'Me, nope.'

Kevin looked surprised. He couldn't see anyone else nearby within range of a psst.

'I don't want you, but King Albert does. You are to follow me.'

And with that the meerkat turned, dropped on to all fours and darted down the path. Kevin had difficulty keeping up with the little animal and had to run as fast as he could. By the time he got to the lion enclosure he was struggling to breathe and had to take big gasps of air as he bent forward and leaned on the fence.

'Kevin!'

A loud voice boomed beside him and as he looked up he saw the majestic face and mane of Albert the lion, who was less than a metre away. Kevin had never been that close to a lion before and felt a rush of fear run from his tummy to the top of his head.

'Oy, you are supposed to bow to the king, mate.'

Kevin hadn't noticed the meerkat was beside him.

'Oh yes, S-sorry, It's just I didn't know that you... Well, um, uh, I've never really met a lion or a king before and I, um...'

Kevin decided it was time to stop talking and do as he had been instructed. He bowed with a flourish waving his arm in front of him like someone in a pantomime might do. There was a little snigger from the meerkat at his feet. As Kevin stood up he could hear the deep breath of the lion.

'Kevin, I understand that you have been talking to some of the animals here. You may not have been aware, but it is forbidden for the animals to talk to humans.'

Kevin felt another wave of fear running through his body.

'I, I, I...'

He couldn't think what to say. What do you say to a lion, a king who is telling you off?

'Please don't eat me,' he finally spluttered.

'Kevin, you have much to learn about the animals in this park. First and foremost, I will not eat you.'

Kevin felt his whole body relax. He had never been so frightened and then so relieved in all his life. Now as he looked at the formidable animal he could sense the power, but also a great peace and wisdom.

'Despite the rules being broken, I wish to thank you for your help in saving the little monkey the other day'

'That's OK, I didn't really do much, I just told Tom and he...'

'Sometimes it is how we do things, not what we do. When the animals were first brought here many of them had very poor experiences of humans. The animal kingdom is full of the stories of how humans and animals once communicated freely until humans destroyed our habitats and killed us for sport. Animals have naturally come to the conclusion that humans are a bad thing and to be avoided, apart from those animals like dogs and cats who have decided to give up their animal language to live with humans.'

Kevin hadn't considered pets could talk or even that they had chosen not to talk as a way to make friends with humans. The mighty lion continued to talk, as he walked backwards and forwards in front of Kevin.

'When animals first came here, though, we were able to trust one human, Cecil Collingwood. He was able to talk to the animals and they were able to find a way of living well together. When his spirit left this life his skills were also lost. Talking to humans became a myth.'

He stopped walking and moved closer to the fence, so he could look deeply into Kevin's eyes.

'You are the first person to understand us for more than 50 years, which has caused something of a problem.'

Kevin was desperately trying to take all this in. He wasn't the only one who could understand the animals, it had been done before, so he wasn't going mad. This was another great relief.

'As you were able to help us the other day, I have decided to lift the ban of speaking to you. The animals will be able to talk with you, if they wish, and in return maybe you will be able to help us again, but Kevin...'

The lion's nose was just an arm's length away and Kevin could see every hair on his magnificent face.

'This is not something that you can tell anyone. Sadly, there are too many humans who would not understand and may try to persuade you to do things for their own gains, not the welfare of the animals. Do you understand?'

'Yes, of course, sir, your majesty, thank you. Wow, that's amazing, I...'

'Now go. It seems that you are attracting someone's interest.'

With that the lion turned and walked slowly along the edge of the enclosure. As Kevin watched him go, he saw Harry surveying him suspiciously, although intermittently, as his attention was drawn between Kevin and the TV crew who were unpacking heavy boxes of equipment from their van.

Chapter
30

'And finally tonight.'

The news reader was shuffling her papers on the TV screen as though trying to get everyone's attention in case they had dropped off to sleep during the last story about a local politician doing something he shouldn't have done.

'Collingwood's Wildlife Emporium has a new resident.'

Kevin looked up.

'Mum, Dad, come and see. Look! It's where I work.'

'A rare Amur leopard from Eastern Russia has just arrived as part of an international breeding project. These amazing big cats, whose numbers have dwindled to the point of extinction in the wild, are slowly growing in number in captivity. After her long journey from Vladivostok Zoo, the new resident at the Emporium was rather reluctant to show her face today.'

There was some video of the park and some blurry pictures of visitors waving. The newsreader continued.

'Owner of the park, Thaddeus Collingwood, was excited about her arrival.'

The pictures then showed Mr. Collingwood talking to the reporter. Kevin could she Shanice scribbling on her note pad in the background and behind her the enclosure where Fefina had been housed. Kevin could also see Harry's head bobbing up and down in the background, clearly checking everything was going well.

'This is a great day for all of us at the Emporium and one my grandfather would have been proud of. He was very much an advocate of the role of conservation for wildlife parks and to think that we now have two of the world's most endangered leopards is just amazing. We can only keep our fingers crossed now for the patter of tiny paws, that would be "purrfect".'

At this point Colly began to laugh at his own joke, throwing his arms out hitting the microphone the reporter was holding and making the camera man duck. The result was an amusing shot of Colly's sandals and rainforest-patterned socks.

Back in the TV studio the two news readers looked amused.

'Another dangerous beast at the Emporium.'

'Yes,' agreed the other presenter, 'and that's just the owner.'

The two of them laughed together and then said their cheesy farewells.

Kevin looked at his parents; they were both reading. Dad was immersed in a book about Second World War fighter planes and Mum was flicking through her magazine. No one seemed the slightest bit interested in the events that were happening at the park.

'Ooh, Marjorie, look at this one.'

Josie came quickly into the room gazing at her phone.

'Look at his profile. Successful businessman, young at heart, loves animals, cups of tea and walking in nature, what do you think? Should I contact him?'

She waved her phone under her sister's nose, a big beaming smile stretching across her face as she did.

'Oh, Josie, you now I don't understand those dating appliances or whatever they are called.'

'Well, I have a feeling about this one. I'm going to say yes.'

And with that she ran out of the room like a schoolgirl rushing to a boyband concert.

Kevin sat quietly. Life seemed to be carrying on pretty much the same as always, and yet he had just had the most amazing experience ever. He could talk to the animals. Yes! He could talk to the animals, just imagine, chatting to a chimp in chimpanzee. As he said those words to himself, he had a strange sense of having heard them somewhere before.

Chapter
31

In contrast to the indifference of the Doolittle family, the Collingwoods and their staff seemed buoyant the next day. There was a great deal of chatter about the local TV coverage and Shanice was now talking to the BBC wildlife team about more filming. As a result, there was lots of gossip about which famous TV star would be coming.

Kevin was assigned to litter picking for the day, which he didn't mind. It meant he could get around the whole park and see all the animals. Kevin thought he'd start by the giraffes. It wasn't long before Jeffrey trotted excitedly over to the fence on his long wobbly legs.

'Mum said I could talk to you now. Isn't that amazing?'

Kevin smiled and agreed, but after the initial excitement they both just stared at each other. Now they could have a conversation they had no idea what to say. What do humans and animals discuss? Kevin usually spoke to his mates about computer games or

You Tube videos he had seen, on rare occasions even football, but that didn't seem to be much use now he was speaking to a giraffe.

'Um, nice weather today,' he said finally and cringed.

That was the sort of thing old people said when they met someone. Jeffrey looked bemused.

'Is there such a thing as nice weather? It just seems like weather to me. I noticed that when it rains you humans change your skin. How do you do that?'

Now it was Kevin's turn to be bemused.

'We don't change our skin.'

'When it was raining the other day your skin was black with a blue pattern; today your skin is green, like the keepers.'

Kevin looked down at his skin or rather the green T-shirt he was wearing and finally understood.

'Oh, you mean our clothes.' He pulled at his t-shirt. 'This isn't skin, it's clothes. Humans wear them to protect them from the cold, rain and sun. Our skin is like this.'

He pulled up his t-shirt to reveal his little belly. He turned around so the giraffe could see it went all the way around. It was as he was spinning around that he noticed Harry and Brutus walking towards him. Kevin stopped. A mixture of fear and embarrassment was now making his cheeks go bright red.

'That's enough of that, whatever it is you are doing, boy.'

'I am collecting rubbish,' Kevin replied, grabbing his bag and litter picking stick.

Harry stood in front of him, as though he was a sergeant major in the army. He looked Kevin up and down and then over his shoulder to where the little giraffe was bending down spreading its long legs so it could nibble on the fresh grass.

'I don't know what it is about you, boy, but there is definitely something odd going on. Go on, move on, there doesn't seem to be any more litter here,' and with that he shoved Kevin in the direction of Big Cat Territory.

Kevin followed a line of fizzy drink cans, empty crisp packets and more Maoam wrappers along the path. When he finally looked up he saw he was next to Fyodor's enclosure. The big cat was pacing back and forth, his gaze fixed on the ground, appearing to be lost in thoughts about something important. Summoning all his courage Kevin cleared his voice with a little cough.

'Are you OK? You look like something is bothering you.'

The fantastic beast stopped, turned towards Kevin and then sank on to its haunches with an almost perceivable sigh.

'You can talk to me,' said Kevin. 'King Albert said it was all right.'

The leopard raised its head and looked straight into

Kevin's eyes. For a brief moment Kevin could feel the power of the animal and almost imagine what it was like to be able to run and hunt in the wild, and then in a flash the feeling was gone.

'I am not sure what a human cub could know or say that would be of any help.'

The leopard spoke with what sounded like an Eastern European accent – or was it the leopard's natural growl that came through on the consonants he was using?

'I might not know how to help, but I do know lots of people I could ask. My mum always says it's not what you know, but who you know, although I think that is more about her trying to get me to go out with Mrs. Harrow's daughter, like that's ever going to happen.'

Kevin realised he was probably saying too much, but the leopard appeared interested.

'You know about dating, young Kevin? Mm.'

The big cat paused, then staring intently again, said, 'Maybe you can tell me how to win the heart of a female.'

Kevin was a little shocked, to say the least. His first day talking to the animals and this mighty beast is asking him about dating. What was worse was that Kevin had no idea about dating, except how he tried to avoid having conversations like that.

'Who...' Kevin's voice came out strangely high pitched and he cleared his throat and tried again, trying to make his voice appear deeper and more mature. 'Who are you trying to date?' he enquired in as relaxed a way as possible.

'Our new princess. Who else could it be?' responded Fyodor with a frustrated tone.

'The princess? Oh, you mean the new leopard that came in yesterday, her name is Fefina I think.'

'Yes, Princess Fefina. She was brought here to be my mate, but she does not even look at me. I do not know what to do.'

With his last comment he sank to the floor on his haunches, his head bowed.

'Well, I am sure it is just that everything is new and different for her. My Auntie Josie is always on dates and says you have to be yourself, but she has been herself for 20 years and still hasn't got a, um...' he struggled to think of the right word here and settled for '...mate. Actually, maybe that's not such good advice. Have you asked anyone else?'

The big cat scoffed at this suggestion.

'I am Fyodor from the Russian Amur dynasty. I do not ask other animals how to win a mate, but you are a human boy who maybe could ask them for me, no?'

Putting the word 'no' on the end of the sentence confused Kevin for a while, until he realised it was actually meant to be a yes and a way of checking that Kevin would help.

'Yeah, I guess I could.'

'Good, then come to me tomorrow with the answer,' and with that the leopard turned away and bounded deep into his enclosure.

Chapter
32

After that start to the day Kevin was sure nothing more could possibly happen, but he noticed Harry's bunion was still giving him a lot of pain as the guard limped across to the office dragging poor Brutus behind. The little dog had been eager to play chase with a group of pigeons who were cooing to each other and dancing around in circles on the lawn in front of the cafeteria. He had now realised that the game was not going to happen and had given in to the tug of his lead

'Ah, Kevin, there you are. Doing a good job I see.'

Colly came bounding up to him with a strange looking tubby man in tow. The man was wearing a grey suit with a stripped blue shirt and pink tie. His thinning hair was scraped over to one side and little beady eyes peered out of some Harry Potter-shaped glasses.

'This is Mr. Tripp, our Health and Safety Officer from the council, just giving us our yearly inspection. I was just saying how important it is to keep the ground clean and tidy.'

'Oh, hi'

'I see you are not wearing any safety gloves,' Mr. Tripp said in a nasally voice and scribbled something on his pad. Colly looked concerned like a rabbit frozen in the headlights of a passing car.

'You forgot these, Kevin.' Tom had appeared, apparently from nowhere, carrying some gloves. 'Mr. Collingwood, would you like me to take Mr. Tripp through the reptile house?'

Colly nodded his approval and Tom escorted the man away, much to Colly's relief.

'I don't know what it is, but when Health and Safety come to inspect I always worry something terrible is going to happen.'

'Are your feet hurting, too?' enquired Kevin, joking.

'Hm, what? No. In fact, Kevin, I am feeling in tiptop condition. I've got a date later.'

A date! Kevin was shocked and intrigued at the same time. Here was a chance for him to help Fyodor.

'How did you get a date?' he enquired.

'Oh, there's this app I use on my phone, very handy for older people like me. I've been matched with someone who is apparently 98% compatible. Amazing what they can do with technology. Well, must be off, its teatime and Mrs. Ainsley won't wait, you know.'

An app. That really wasn't the answer Kevin wanted. After all, not many leopards have smartphones.

'Oy, look it's Dozy Doolittle!'

Kevin's heart sank; he recognised that voice. Dean Bishop, the school bully and trainee thug, was waddling towards him, cracking his knuckles as he got closer.

''Ere, shouldn't you be inside one of the cages, not out here with the humans?'

He laughed loudly at his own joke, which encouraged his two buddies to join in. They all pushed past Kevin, nudging him with their shoulders as they went, causing him to fall over and land on his bag of rubbish.

'Yeah, that's where you belong, in the trash,' called back Dean, his comments punctuated by more hearty laughs from his sidekicks.

Picking himself up Kevin got back to his litter picking, adding sandwich wrappers, a milk carton and several ice-cream wrappers to his rapidly filling bag. What happened next was all rather a blur.

Tom came running past speaking rapidly into his walkie-talkie and shouting, 'Stay there, Kevin.'

Other keepers were also running in the same direction and Kevin could see Mr. Collingwood hurrying the Health and Safety man in the opposite direction to the café. Now, Kevin knew he should do as he was told, but when adrenaline runs through your body you either run away, play dead or fight. Kevin could feel his adrenaline saying 'Don't run away, fight,' so he dropped his rubbish bag and ran after the keepers.

Luckily, there were few people around when they stopped in Big Cat Territory. At this time of the day visitors tended to watch the penguins being fed, but today it looked like it was time for the tiger to be fed. Dean Bishop and his mates were stood still, knees visibly knocking. Around them at a distance were Tom and the keepers. Tom was shouting instructions to them to stay calm and still. In front of them was Gnasha. Kevin darted around the back of the enclosures to get a better look. Gnasha was roaring, but Kevin could make out some words from the scary sound.

'They threw a rock at my head, they threw a rock at my head.'

As Kevin looked, he could see a trickle of blood oozing from Gnasha's forehead. Kevin could see one of the keepers fiddling with what looked like a rifle. Clearly all the keepers were petrified, but Kevin could hear the roar of the tiger. This was a mixture of anger and pain. Everyone else just saw the anger and were afraid, their minds planning what they could do – even kill the tiger, if they had to. From behind him Kevin heard another voice. This one was gentle. There was a smoothness in the tones and a very strong Eastern European accent not unlike Fyodor's. As he turned to look, he saw the silhouette of Fefina against the sun.

'Do not be afraid, little one. That tiger has no teeth.

He is just teaching those boys a lesson they won't forget.'

Kevin turned back to the scene in front of him. The keeper with the gun had moved beside Dean and raised it to his shoulder and was taking aim at the tiger. Without thinking, Kevin ran past the tiger towards the group of boys, and for a second he caught the tiger's eye.

'Go!' he shouted.

The keeper with the gun pointed it down to the ground, allowing Kevin to run past. When he raised the gun again, Gnasha had turned and was running back into his enclosure. Tom shouted an instruction to secure the cage, then grabbed Kevin.

'What do you think you were doing? I said stay away.'

'I'm sorry, Tom, but the tiger was hurt. Those boys threw a rock at him; he is bleeding.'

Tom's anger seemed to disappear. He turned to Dean and the boys.

'Right, you lot, with me.'

He grabbed Dean by the collar and nodded to two of the other keepers to do the same, and together they marched them off towards the security gate.

As Kevin walked back to the office, he saw Colly laughing jovially with the health inspector and ushering him into the car. He waved enthusiastically as the car drove away before turning to Tom who had left the boys with a jubilant Harry, who was talking to them loudly while walking back and forth wagging his finger, obviously enjoying the moment.

Kevin was close enough to overhear Colly say, 'Phew, I think we got away with that one, Tom. What on earth happened?'

'Well, it seems the boys may have thrown a rock at old Gnasha. I understand he might be hurt, so I've called the vet. Our new keeper Sam may have also accidently left the keepers' entrance to the enclosure unlocked, so Gnasha was able to get out.'

'OK. Sam, you say? Pull him in for a chat and let's think what we can tell the press. This is sure to get out. Shanice is going to have a meltdown.'

With that they both hurried towards the office.

As Kevin looked back towards the office, Harry was still giving Dean Bishop a serious telling off. The boys all looked terrified and Kevin couldn't help enjoying the moment for a few seconds. Sitting on the roof of the security hut were two woodpigeons, the same ones Brutus had been eager to play with earlier. Kevin smiled as he heard their now familiar coo.

'You're so silly, so, sooo silly.'

Chapter
33

Kevin appeared for breakfast. Mum had obviously felt he needed feeding up, as the veggie sausages were replaced by bacon and eggs, which were being dished up as Kevin arrived in the kitchen. A boy band was playing on the radio and it must have been an old song, because his mum was doing the little dance she always did. It looked more like she had an itch she couldn't scratch rather than any serious dance moves, but then she was washing up and a full Strictly Come Dancing routine would not have been practical. The band got to the chorus and Mum joined in. It sounded like she was singing about tiger feet. Really, thought Kevin. How could parents complain about modern songs when the old ones were about 'tiger feet'? The song did, however, remind him about the previous day's events. He hadn't told his parents what had happened, as he was convinced that they would try to stop him working in the wildlife park.

'Morning, sunshine,' Dad said jovially and ruffled his

son's hair. As loving as it was, it still annoyed Kevin who had spent considerable time getting his hair to stand up in the right places, so his ears didn't look too big.

'Did you sleep well, darling?' Mum enquired. 'I hope Josie didn't wake you when she came in. It was very late.' She exchanged a knowing look with Dad and added with a smile, 'It must have been a good date.'

Talking about his auntie's love life was not on the list of things Kevin had planned for the morning. He rather impolitely shovelled in his breakfast and headed for the door.

'Is that how the animals eat in that zoo of yours?' his mum called after him, tutting as she put his plate in the sink; she always washed the plates straight away before she put them in the dishwasher.

All the staff had been called to the office for a meeting that morning and Kevin was included. Mr. Collingwood had prepared a number of sketches on a flipchart and was using a breadstick to point out important information. Breadsticks aren't particularly designed for public speaking and pointing at diagrams. As a result, there was a growing pile of broken bits around Colly's feet that he kept standing on, with a noticeable crunch.

There was a thorough review of what happened the day before. It seemed the boys had confessed to throwing a rock, so they had been banned from the park and their parents informed. Luckily, the tiger had not been seriously hurt and the boys only frightened. The big issue for the staff was how the gate to the enclosure could have been left open. While Sam had been responsible at the time, he was adamant he had not left it open and after much debate there was still uncertainty about what happened. Also luckily, the Health and Safety Officer had not seen anything and had gone away fairly happy with things.

There was one other item for discussion. Tom raised concerns that the two leopards did not seem to be showing any interest in each other. They had now been able to share an enclosure and everyone had rather hoped that there would be an instant attraction, but instead they seemed to be staying as far away from each other as possible. Shanice at this point spoke about the interest from TV companies and how much the park could make if the leopards were to one day have a cub. All this seemed a little presumptuous, thought Kevin. The staff had started to get a bit bored and were giggling amongst themselves.

Then one said, a little too loudly, 'Maybe Colly should give them a few dating tips.'

Colly seemed to take this rather well. He turned to the rather cheeky staff member and waggled his crumbling bread stick at him.

'I'll have you know that's not a bad idea, since yours truly had a rather successful date last night.'

'Eugh, please,' said Shanice, in a rather discouraging

way.

The meeting was dismissed amid the laughter that followed.

Tom kept Kevin busy the rest of the day carrying food, bedding and a large amount of elephant dung from one location to another. Although he was working hard, the jobs helped to get Kevin around almost all the park. This meant that he was able to speak to many of the animals. He was surprised at how delighted most of them had been to spend a few minutes chatting and appeared to enjoy telling him about how they had got to know their mates. For some of them it was a long story and reminded him of the stories his grandmother used to tell him about how she met his granddad at an old-fashioned tea dance when she had stepped on his foot.

By the time the day ended, Kevin had quite a few bits of information for Fyodor and he headed back to Big Cat Territory. Fefina was at the front of the enclosure.

'Ah, the brave little human who saved the fearsome tiger,' she said, as he approached.

'I'm not brave. I just didn't want Gnasha being shot when it wasn't his fault. Thanks for telling me he had no teeth, though. I didn't realise he was harmless.'

The leopard winked at him.

Oh, he's not harmless or toothless. I just said that so you would stop being afraid and do something.'

'What!' snapped back Kevin. 'You mean he could have attacked me? I could have been tiger fodder.'

The leopard laughed.

'The thing is, you weren't, were you? You acted bravely. I like that.'

The leopard then snarled. Out of the corner of her eye she had seen Fyodor approaching and turned to walk away from him.

Kevin moved along the fence to where Fyodor was waiting.

'You were talking to the princess,' he growled.

'Yes,' said Kevin 'I can't believe she tricked me yesterday.'

'What did you find out for me?'

'Well,' Kevin said, taking his phone out of his pocket to read the notes he had made about his conversations. He cleared his throat as if he was addressing the school assembly.

'Trumpeter swans blow bubbles, bow and sing to each other when they are finding a mate.'

Fyodor's expression of hope seemed to change suddenly into disbelief.

'You expect me to blow bubbles and sing?'

'Well, maybe not that one, but these are just some ideas,' Kevin continued. 'I spoke to the coyotes. They like grooming, wrestling, chasing each other and bumping hips.'

Fyodor looked unimpressed, but Kevin plodded on

through his notes.

'Snapping turtles face each other, then sway their heads, the male penguins give their females a rock for their nest building, um, oh yes, and the hooded seals blow up their faces.'

'Anything else?' said Fyodor dejectedly.

Kevin couldn't think of anything, but decided he ought to say something.

'Well, the woodpigeons seem to say to each other that they are silly.'

That was exactly how Kevin was feeling now. Thinking about the things he had just said to the leopard he now felt silly indeed.

'Well, they are just examples that seem to work for other animals. You could give them a try.'

Kevin wasn't sure if leopards could feel fed up, but that is what Fyodor looked like, and the large sigh he made didn't fill Kevin with any confidence that he had helped the situation.

'OK, well, sorry if that isn't much help. I'll see what else I can find out.'

Kevin left the leopard and made his was back through the park. At the gate, Harry was talking to another man in the same security uniform.

'You need to keep an eye on the youngsters around here; they are always up to something.'

'Hi,' said Kevin on his way past.

'This is Sergei. He will be in charge while I have a

few days off, my lad.'

'Are you going on holiday?'

'I, my lad,' Harry paused for effect, 'am going to the International Society of Security Officers annual conference in Brighton. I had a special invitation. I'm going to find out how to improve the security of this place so I can keep my eye on everyone.'

With that, he gave Kevin one of his 'I'm watching you' looks. Kevin hadn't minded these before, but now he was talking to the animals he knew he had a secret to keep and it worried him somewhat. A flash of guilt appeared on his face, his cheeks reddening slightly. Feeling uncomfortable, Kevin hurried through the gate, hoping Harry hadn't noticed. When he looked back the new guard was watching him carefully and Kevin had a strange sense of uneasiness that lasted all the way home.

Chapter
34

'Ooh, ooh, he sent me another message.'

Kevin had not seen his auntie like this before. She was usually quite laid back about things, but ever since her date she was excited about everything and kept reading out slushy messages from her mystery man. Apparently, the date had gone well, even when he had accidently knocked over a glass of water, causing a waterfall off the table and soaking their sandaled feet.

As Josie read out another message where she was called 'cutie pie' twice, Kevin made a face at Dad like he was going to be sick; Dad laughed, doing the same back. They both made their way into the kitchen and attempted to have a manly conversation about football, but since neither of them were particularly interested in the game they fell silent for a bit, just enjoying the quiet.

'Dad, how do you know what to say to someone if you want to go on a date?'

'Oh, I see. Have your eye on someone, do you? Is it

that girl at the zoo you were on about?'

'No, it's just a friend of mine.'

Dad looked at him with a knowing smile as if to say, 'This is you and not really a friend', which actually in this case was wrong.

'He likes someone, but doesn't know what to say.'

'Mm.'

Dad was thoughtful. He hadn't planned on having this conversation with Kevin for a while and wasn't really prepared. Besides that it had been 25 years since he asked his wife out on a date and, if he was honest, he had no idea what he'd said.

'I think it's probably a good idea not to try to impress anyone with thinking of clever things to say. Hello is usually a good first step. Be polite then ask some questions and most importantly take time to listen to the answers.'

He stopped, feeling quite chuffed with his answer. Kevin was mildly impressed, too.

'Thanks, Dad.'

With that, he headed off to his room.

'Are you not going to tell me who it is, then?' Dad called after him.

'No. I said, it was for a friend.'

'OK, I get it, mum's the word.'

Clearly, thought Kevin, he doesn't get it, but then even if I told him all the truth, he wouldn't get it either.

Chapter
35

Kevin had great difficulty getting time to visit Fyodor the next day. The new guard seemed to be more watchful than Harry and although he was very friendly, saying 'Good morning' in his strong accent at every opportunity, even in the afternoon, Kevin still had an uneasy feeling about him.

When he finally got to the leopard enclosure if was nearly closing time. Fyodor looked fed up and was slumped on his haunches under the tree staring aimlessly at the floor.

'Hi, Fyodor,' Kevin said with his best 'cheer up' voice. 'Any news?'

'Well, I think we can safely say that the blowing up my face, singing and giving her a rock worked as well as I thought they would.'

Kevin wasn't sure if that was good news or not.

'I think it is fair to say that Fefina now thinks I am a complete idiot and hasn't been anywhere near me all day.'

'Maybe you shouldn't try and think of clever things to say. Just say hello, be polite and ask questions to show you're interested and listen to what she says.'

Kevin couldn't believe he had just repeated what Dad said, almost word for word. He had only just finished speaking when Fefina walked between them, swishing her long-spotted tail as she went. Her pale, patterned fur seemed to glow in the sunlight.

'Hi, Fefina, you look beautiful,' said Kevin, without even thinking.

The leopard stopped and her brown eyes met his.

'Thank you and hello to you, little one. It is nice to be appreciated.'

She turned her head to Fyodor as she said the last few words and with another flick of the tail leaped across the enclosure, where she stretched her body up against the tree, drawing her claws down the trunk.

'You are right, Kevin, she is beautiful and I love watching her sharpening her claws like that. Maybe I should just take things slowly and be polite.'

Kevin thought this was probably a good time to leave and wandered back across the now deserted park to sign out. The visitors had left and the staff were all making their way home. There had been no sign of Colly for much of the day; Kevin had only caught a glimpse of him walking across the park looking at his phone and occasionally bumping into chairs, trees and old ladies.

The security gate looked busy though. A large truck was at the barrier. Inside, two men wearing sunglasses were talking to Sergei in a language Kevin didn't understand. The new guard beamed another 'Good morning!' 'to Kevin as he passed. The truck was white with 'Animal Food Internationale' on the side. The driver revved the engine just as Kevin was squeezing past the truck. The noise made him lose his balance and he toppled towards the vehicle, his hands landing on the side with a bang. A head appeared out of the window of the cab and glared in disgust. Kevin apologised and quickly left the park. As he walked away he noticed his hand felt sticky. He looked down and saw it was covered in white paint.

The truck moved off and drove slowly through the park. It took the road to Big Cat Territory where it pulled off the road and around behind the keepers' storage sheds amongst the trees. The driver stopped the engine. Both men sat there in silence, waiting.

Chapter 36

Mum was waiting at the door when Kevin arrived home. She was tutting and tapping her foot, which was a sure sign she was upset about something. Sure enough, she was.

'Where have you been? We are going to be late, it's the singing concert tonight and we are meeting Susan and her daughter Charlotte.'

'Mum, I said I didn't want to sing in that stupid concert,' Kevin replied angrily.

'I know, darling, so I arranged for you to come and watch. I said you could keep Charlotte company. She would like that; she's a lovely girl. Now, get out of those smelly clothes and into your smart jeans as quick as a flash. We need to go.'

Kevin knew that there was no arguing with his mum over this, however awful the evening sounded. He went through the motions of getting changed and, rather than showering, he sprayed half a can of deodorant under his arms and on his clothes so that by the time he walked downstairs there was a musky haze following him. With a cough, a splutter and a weary smile his mum ushered him into the car.

Chapter
37

As the early evening succumbed to the shadows of dusk, the two men in the truck at Big Cat Territory became more animated. A phone rang and a brief message stirred them into action. They moved to the rear of their vehicle and opened the doors. Inside were two large cages. They dragged them to the tail gate and lowered them to the ground with an elongated whirr and a large clunk. They looked around cautiously. The park was empty except for Sergei who was marching purposefully towards them barking orders. There was an exchange in their language and together they walked toward the leopard enclosure, one of them carrying a large bucket of meat.

Chapter
38

The concert Kevin was having to endure was in his school hall. Being in school during the summer holidays, whatever the reason, just felt wrong, but especially when he was being forced to sit by Charlotte Harrow. She was a nice enough girl, but she was very clever: so clever that the other children in the class used to make fun of her for always answering the teacher's questions. She was a bit like Hermione Grainger from the Harry Potter books, but not quite as rebellious. Now that they were sitting in the school hall, Charlotte seemed compelled to talk about history and had started on about Tudor England and the importance of Anne Boleyn's short reign as Queen.

Kevin had started to daydream, which was his usual solution to boring lessons, and was looking out of the nearby window. From where he sat he could just make out the trees around the wildlife park in the distance and he began imagining himself conducting a concert in the park, introducing animals as they came on stage to sing various musical numbers. He started to think of which songs the animals could sing. Obviously Albert the lion would sing Katy Perry's 'Roar' and...

Chapter 39

The three men stood near the leopard enclosure and the one carrying the bucket took out a piece of steak, Sergei watched as the other covered the steak in some power and rubbed it in. Then he repeated this with three other pieces of meat before hurling them over the fence. The activity of the men and the smell of the meat had brought the leopards to the edge of their enclosure. One piece of steak landed at Fyodor's feet. He sniffed it. It smelt slightly unusual, but the meatiness was enough to make him take a bite. Fefina had devoured the pieces that landed near her and she was looking for more. Fyodor was uncertain though. After the first bite the taste was troubling him.

'Are you not eating that then?' Fefina said as she approached the last piece of meat.

'No. Wait. Don't you think it tastes funny?'

'All your food here tastes funny to me,' Fefina scoffed moving closer to the juicy steak.

Fyodor snatched the meat away from her. She had

stopped and was looking at him in a strange, almost sleepy way.

'You know, you are quite handsome,' she said. 'I didn't notice at first, but you... you...'

Her voice had changed and she seemed to be in slow motion. Fyodor watched as the female leopard slumped to the ground breathing heavily. He nuzzled against her, but she was sound asleep. Fyodor looked at the men by the fence. They were smiling. As he watched they started to appear blurry and slowly his vision narrowed like he was in a tunnel getting ever narrower until he, too, slumped to the floor, his eyes closed.

From his enclosure just metres away Gnasha had seen everything.

With a growl he leaped to the fence roaring, 'Danger!'

The three men, startled at first by the roar, soon felt safe enough to poke fun at the tiger before continuing with their plan.

Chapter
40

In the stuffy school hall there was a group of seven-year-olds on stage singing, 'I just can't wait to be king'. Kevin was thinking about the film The Lion King, which he loved, and then the warthog character, Pumbaa, then strangely he started to think of his English teacher, Mrs. Francis. In his head, Mrs. Francis now started tap-dancing, her feet tippety-tapping on the floor. The tapping got louder and louder until Kevin realised that it was coming from outside.

He looked to the window and there, tapping on the glass next to him, was one of the woodpigeons that flew around all day saying everyone was silly. It was looking directly at him and seemed to be trying to get his attention. Even if this was just a coincidence, it did seem like a chance to get away from the singing, which was now getting so shrill Kevin was afraid the glass would start shattering. He made an excuse he was going to the toilet and shuffled through his row of spectators, standing on feet, handbags and small children before he could make his way out of the hall.

As soon as he was in the open air he was surrounded by six pigeons, all were cooing the same thing.

'Yooou, Zoo, Yooou, Zooo.'

Whilst cooing the pigeons began shooing. They flapped their wings almost as if they were trying to direct Kevin towards the exit. The pigeons might not have the best vocabulary, but this message 'Yooou, Zooo' was pretty clear. With the birds in hot pursuit, Kevin broke into a run and headed back to the wildlife park.

Chapter 41

Inside the park, the activities of the three men had caused quite a commotion amongst the animals. All of them were screeching, squawking, growling and in the case of the hyenas laughing at the men's attempts to drag the unconscious leopards from the enclosure and into the cages by their truck. The men were all sweating with the effort of carrying such large animals, so much so that their foreheads shone in the truck's headlights.

As Kevin ran into the park he was surrounded by the most deafening noise from the animals. He felt his heart pounding in his chest, which seemed to send a throbbing into his head. He rushed to the nearest enclosure and saw Jeffrey running about on his wobbly legs. Towering above him his mother was calling out instructions. From her viewpoint 3 metres above everyone else she could see what was happening and was narrating for all the other animals.

'Mum says that some men are taking the leopards. What are you going to do?'

Kevin was shocked.

'Me? I don't know what to do. Don't you need to be a secret agent or something? I'm just a boy.'

The little giraffe looked at him with his big brown eyes and said, 'You're a Kevin and the only hope we have.'

The noise of the animals was increasing. Kevin's brain was whirring. They were expecting him to do something to stop some bad guys stealing two leopards. The whole situation seemed more than Kevin could manage, but just as he felt like giving up an idea flashed out of the dark corners of his brain. It whizzed around a bit trying to get Kevin to notice it, and when he did it stopped to unveil its plan.

Kevin suddenly remembered where Tom kept the emergency walkie-talkies and he headed for the offices. They were unlocked; in fact, everything seemed to be open. That new guard certainly was not doing his job. Kevin grabbed a walkie-talkie and tried calling for help. He repeated his messages pressing every button he could find and switching to every channel. On channel 5 he heard a crackle then Tom's voice.

'Hi, who's that?'

'Tom, it's Kevin. I'm at the park. Some men are taking the leopards. You need to get here now and bring the army or MI5 or something.'

'Kevin, what the... Why are... What? Never mind. I'm coming in. Don't do anything silly.'

The last line may not have had the desired effect, because Kevin had seen the master keys hanging on a peg and had come up with another idea. This one was either a brilliant plan, or one that was going to get him into a whole heap of trouble. Oh well, he thought, there's only one way to find out.

With that he grabbed the keys and headed to the lion enclosure. Kevin's plan was to make his own army.

Chapter 42

As the cage door swung open, Kevin was aware of the majesty of the lion as he jumped past him. He could have let this moment last a lifetime but he didn't really have that much time.

'I'm going to let the animals out. Can you get them to stop the truck?'

The lion roared, 'Thank you Kevin, but no! You are too slow. Give the keys to the macaques. They can get to everyone much quicker than you and without being seen. You go to the main gate and make sure the truck can't leave.'

Kevin ran to the macaque enclosure, unfastened the door and repeated the instructions to the little monkeys, who were out and on their mission within seconds.

In Big Cat Territory, the three men were aware of the noise and commotion around them and were feeling uneasy. They were hurrying now and getting in each other's way as a result. They eventually managed to get the sleeping bodies of both Fyodor and Fefina into the cages and on to the back of the lorry. They closed the door and all three squeezed into the cab. As the driver turned the key in the ignition, his colleagues began shouting instructions to hurry. The engine stuttered and chugged, but failed to start. The shouts of the other men got louder and more frantic until the driver shouted back. The men fell quiet. As the driver turned his head back to the road he understood the reason for his colleagues' silence. Just ahead on the truck, and snarling, was the king of the beasts.

The driver tried again with renewed effort to start the truck. At the fifth attempt it spluttered into life, sending a plume of black choking smoke from the exhaust. The driver stamped on the accelerator, making the wheels spin and throwing stones and dirt into the growing black cloud. The truck jumped forward and swerved past the lion. It headed for the exit, but then suddenly screamed to a halt. In front of the three men this time was Gnasha, baring his full set of sparkling teeth, which glinted in the trucks headlights. The driver threw the truck into reverse, then spun the wheels again to avoid the approaching tiger. The truck hit the kerb and its wheels slid and gripped at the grass on the roadside. The bump sent the sleeping bodies of the leopards into the air. They landed with a thud and Fyodor's eye lid twitched open.

As the truck made its bumpy way across the grass

under the trees, there was another surprise for the men inside. Swinging from the branches, the monkeys landed on the truck and set about removing the windscreen wipers and anything else they could grab hold of. Swerving as he tried to see through a hoard of furry faces and bare bottoms, the driver forced the truck back on to the road, heading for the rear exit. For a moment there was a sense of relief in the cab of the lorry. Freedom seemed to be in sight. They all began to cheer and chatter excitedly, before they were brought to another screeching halt by three elephants that had stampeded from their enclosure to block the escape route. The driver swore in his native language and violently turned the truck around 180 degrees to go back the way they had come. The driver's face was fixed in an angry glare, his teeth were tightly clenched and his knuckles were turning white as his gripped the steering wheel.

Chapter 43

Kevin was able to follow much of what was happening by listening to the giraffe commentary. To his horror, he realised the truck was heading in his direction. He had found the button that lowered the main barrier and he was stood alone. This was one time he would have welcomed seeing the grumpy face of Harry in the security hut.

The truck was now driving straight towards Kevin. He could feel his nerves leaving his tummy and filling his whole body. His legs were starting to feel like jelly and his heart was beating so fast it sounded like African drums playing. He could see the three men in the truck and recognised one of them as Sergei. The truck was now only metres away. Kevin dived into the hut and closed his eyes. There was nothing more he could do.

The driver was completely focused on his escape. It was just the barrier between them and the main road. His eyes narrowed on the target as though he was aiming a rifle. His foot pushed the accelerator pedal right to the floor. If he had been more aware of his present surroundings, he may have noticed the movement in the cab. Just seconds before they would hit the barrier, the head of a large python appeared between the driver's legs. His reaction was quite normal for anyone facing the flicking tongue of one of the world's largest snakes. He threw his hands in the air, screamed and tried to jump out of the truck. His erratic movements sent the vehicle careering to the left and over a large grass mound. The jolt this time dislodged the cages, throwing them from the back of the truck. Fyodor was thrown to the side and then from the cage as it buckled and split. He remained dazed but awake and his strength was returning.

The truck and its human cargo continued down the bank and into the boating lake at the bottom. There was a splash, then a hiss from the engine, then silence.

On the other side of the lake in a swan-shaped peddle boat, Colly stood up rather unsteadily. He was trying to take in the commotion on the opposite shore when the wave created from the hissing, sinking truck tilted his boat sending him off balance. He landed headfirst in the arms of his date, who giggled childishly then planted a large wet kiss on his lips.

Kevin bravely peeked through his hands, which were covering his face. The picture he saw was unbelievable. Sergei and the other man were trying to drag themselves from the muddy lake. The driver who had jumped from the truck was frantically shouting as animals of all sizes and shapes surrounded him. In his hand he held a gun. The animals moved carefully. They all knew to be afraid of a weapon like that. They knew the dangers of man's deadly creations that had taken the species further and further away from the natural world and the lives they had once all shared together.

The driver was shouting 'Get back' in English, almost as though he expected the animals to understand him better than using his own language, which they did. The man had backed himself towards the cage that Fefina was in. The fall had brought her out of her sleep and she was half sitting in a daze.

In the lake, the hippos had finally arrived and had seen their opportunity to help out while enjoying a muddy bath. They started circling the two men in the water like a synchronised swimming team, their giant mouths yawning wide at every opportunity to add a little show of strength. It was working, as Sergei and the other man seemed frozen in fear.

Fyodor was now on his feet and slowly stalking the driver. His focus was clear; the man was his prey. His tail flicked from side to side behind him, his neck lowered and the power building in his legs. Looking from beast to beast, the driver finally made eye contact with the leopard. He raised his gun, his hand shaking slightly; the leopard was completely still, primed. Kevin was too far away to help this time, but he couldn't help crying out.

'No-o-o-o-o-o!'

His voice seemed to carry on for ever as everything went into slow motion. Kevin could see the bending and release of the leopard's giant leg muscles. He could see the shake and twitch of the driver's hand and he heard the bang of the gun as its force echoed around the park.

Chapter
44

Whilst hurrying down the road, Mrs. Doolittle heard the gunshot. Like most people living in a country where gunshots are few and far between, she dismissed it as an annoying neighbour who was letting off a firework on a night other than 5th November. All she could think of was the telling off Kevin was going to get when she caught up with him. Walking out on Miss Dalrimple's musical extravaganza was not the done thing in polite suburban society.

For some reason Mrs. Doolittle was heading for the wildlife park. She didn't know why, but something inside her was making her go that way. As she hurried along, her handbag banging against her side, she became aware of the sirens. There was the honking of the fire truck, the piercing wail of the ambulance and the scream of the police car and then another and another!

Chapter
45

As the gunshot continued to fade away, many of the smaller animals ran for the safety of their enclosure, leaving the elephants and big cats surrounding the scene. The bullet had found its target and Fyodor lay panting on the ground.

From the lake, Kevin heard the call of his name and he looked over to see Mr. Collingwood frantically waving his arms from his giant swan. Sitting next to him in the boat and pedaling frantically was Auntie Josie. On any other day Kevin might have been confused or even amused seeing his auntie pedaling frantically, her tongue hanging out of the side of her mouth like a panting puppy, but today, with everything else that happening, this seemed rather mundane.

Kevin cautiously made his way to the scene playing before him. Sergei and the other man were still stuck in the lake, with the hippos blocking any attempt to dash to freedom. The driver who had fired the shot had sought safety in the only place he could find, the empty cage that Fyodor had previously been captive in. Fefina was now alert and snarling at him, although she had not been able to escape her prison. Albert was roaring ferociously next to the buckled door of the cage. As he roared, the sounds mixed with the ever-increasing wail of sirens and motors of the emergency services as they drew closer.

Armed police officers, who had been enjoying a nice cup of tea with some biscuits the sergeant had brought in, were now clad in bulletproof vests and helmets, running into the park. The scene before Kevin seemed to be a Hollywood blockbuster movie, and he was in it. He looked away from the lights, sirens and police officers surging through the gate and gazed back at the truck. Albert had disappeared and so had the other animals. All that was left were the caged Fefina and Fyodor, who was lying motionless on the floor, his breathing becoming ever slower.

Like Nelson at the Battle of Trafalgar, Mr. Collingwood stood on his boat shouting orders. He was waving his arms and signalling to the police to arrest the three men. As he did so, he attempted to step elegantly from his wobbling swan and fell headfirst into the muddy brown water. Josie bent over quickly to help, but instead fell on top of him. They both rose from their unexpected bath with a cry of disgust that quickly turned to laughter as they saw themselves, clothes sagging, hair plaited with weeds and slimy, mud-splattered faces. Hand in hand, they slowly trudged up the bank from the lake like some alien beings from Doctor Who.

'Kevin! Kevin... What on earth...?' Mrs. Doolittle had arrived. 'Josie, is that you?'

Her surprise was further increased when a rather portly policeman in his riot gear stopped her from going any further.

'I'm sorry, madam, you can't go in there. Those men may be dangerous.'

'And I may be dangerous if you don't let me see my son,' she replied, pushing the officer aside and grabbing Kevin in one of her bear-like hugs. She was about to do the same with Josie, but after noticing the amount of muddy water that was dripping from her she offered a welcoming smile instead.

Chapter
46

As Kevin sat outside Colly's office the next morning, he went over the events of the night before preparing for the emergency meeting that Mr. Collingwood had called him for. He couldn't believe what happened or, more strangely, he thought, that he didn't seem to be in any trouble. There had been no mention of the fact that a large percentage of the animal residents of the park had been roaming wild and helping to save the leopards from three criminals. When Tom had arrived on the scene, he had quickly called the vet and the other rangers. They had checked everywhere and found that all the animals were locked in their enclosures, including the 7-foot-long python, which had apparently just reappeared after being missing for more than a week.

Kevin watched as Mr. Collingwood finished talking to some reporters. With his usual flair, he tripped over the microphone cable as he said his goodbyes and continued to drag the poor sound man with him as if taking a dog for a walk.

'Ah, Kevin, my boy, good to see you again. Well, what a morning and what a night. Come into the office; there's something I wanted to ask you.'

Mr. Collingwood disentangled himself from the microphone cable with a little skip and a hop and marched towards the office. Kevin followed him feeling a bit like he had been called in to see the head teacher at school. It's funny, he thought, that whenever you go into the head teacher's office you feel like you've done something wrong, even if you know it's just for a chat. Today was the same. He had been told no one was cross with him. In fact, many of the rangers had patted him on the back and ruffled his hair in the way Dad did when he was proud of him.

In the office, Colly parked himself behind his desk and sat back in his chair. He rubbed his hands together a few times, then leaned forward, putting his elbows on the desk and leaning on his intertwined fingers.

'Kevin. Thank you again for your swift thinking last night and for calling Tom. You always seem to be in the right place at the right time.'

He sat back, this time going too far, causing his chair to tip. He changed his balance to correct the possible fall and came tumbling forwards almost banging his head on the desk. Gaining composure, he cleared his voice.

'Huh, hum. What I don't understand, is how did you

know what was happening?'

Kevin looked directly into Mr. Collingwood's big blue eyes and without thinking he found himself telling the whole story from his first day and his chat with the orangutans and then Jeffrey, the meeting with Albert, to the difficult relationship with the leopards ,and his actions unlocking the lion cage, and giving the keys to the little monkeys. The story lasted a good twenty minutes and when he finished he could feel a great sense of relief. He looked away, expecting a laugh of disbelief, but there was not a sound. When he looked back Colly was motionless, his mouth was open, and he appeared to be thinking. He stood up almost in a trance and without saying anything walked to the bookcase. He reached up to the top shelf and after moving aside a few dusty old books he grabbed a leather-bound journal. It was tied with a leather strap and had the initials CC embossed on the front.

'This belonged to my grandfather, Cecil Collingwood,' Colly announced as he opened the book. 'It was his journal. He wrote in it every day and it tells how he started the wildlife park after a trip to Africa in the 1920s. I used to love reading this when I was a boy, because, well, I thought it was just my grandfather's personality, being silly or creative or something, but he used to record the conversations he said he had with the animals. Here, look.'

He opened the journal wide for Kevin to see. The

writing was very neat with elaborate swirls. There were little pictures on the pages, too, drawings of animals and plants.

It said: '20th February 1965. The orangutans were complaining about the water and how it affected their hairstyles.'

'Yes, they still are today,' Kevin found himself saying before he could stop himself.

'And here,' Mr. Collingwood said excitedly. '28th March. Pollyanna the grey parrot led the meeting of the animals who agreed to work together and with me to build the park.'

With that he shut the book and peered over his glasses inquisitively at Kevin.

'You can talk to the animals, like my grandfather did?'

'Uh, yes. I guess so,' Kevin replied, uncertain of what was going to happen if he agreed.

Colly seemed ecstatic.

'That's fantastic, I have tried so hard, but never been able to make any sense of any of them, except those woodpigeons that always seem to be saying "You're so silly, so, sooo silly."'

'Yes, that's what they do say; it's sort of their thing.'

'Well I never. I... do you think...' that is to say, I have always wanted to ask them questions. Is there any way you could translate for me?'

'Well, the thing is, I am not supposed to tell anyone.

I'm not sure they would let me. I could ask.'

'Well, yes, if you could I'm sure we could really change things around here. Let me know.'

With that he clapped his hands together and excitedly busied himself with some papers on his desk. Kevin took that as a cue to leave.

Chapter
47

That night it was Mexican night at home. Auntie Josie had decide to cook and was trying out her special burrito recipe which she had come across on her trip around the Yucatan Peninsula. She seemed very excited and was singing to herself as she mashed up a pile of avocados and tomatoes to make guacamole.

The relaxed atmosphere halted when the doorbell rang. Auntie Josie asked Kevin to get the door and nipped into the toilet to check her hair. Mrs. Doolittle rushed to the kitchen to grab a tea tray and Mr. Doolittle shifted uncomfortably on the sofa as he turned the page of the local newspaper.

Kevin could still see the headlines: 'NO CATNAP FOR COLLINGWOOD'S.'

Kevin opened the door and was surprised to see Colly in a clean white suit, red shirt, orange tie and green shoes and with him Shanice in her hoody and sneakers. Colly gave Kevin a crooked smile and a jaunty handshake, before Auntie Josie eagerly pushed Kevin aside to greet the pair with a hearty 'Hellooo.'

She beamed at Shanice who didn't notice, as she was engrossed in some time-consuming app on her phone. There was an awkward moment with some introductions and a sulky response from Shanice of 'Whatever,' before Auntie Josie escorted her guests towards the dining room. If things weren't odd enough Mrs. Doolittle added to the pot of discomfort by suggesting the teenagers might want to hang out together in the kitchen while the adults headed for the best room. Kevin and Shanice shared a roll of the eyes and headed for the kitchen, where there was an inviting bowl of chips and dips for them to tuck into.

The conversation was hard – well, to be honest, virtually non-existent. They were the same age and worked together, but had never really spoken. Kevin broke the silence with a tut and a face that said 'Adults, huh? What are they like!', which prompted a small smile from Shanice. At that point there was an almighty crash and Mrs. Doolittle ran to the kitchen sink grabbing a bowl, carpet cleaner and kitchen roll.

Kevin looked at Shanice.

Did you bring your dad a spare shirt?'

She laughed pulling a rolled-up t-shirt from her bag.

Chapter
48

The next few weeks went by without too many problems. Shanice and Kevin both agreed that Colly dating Auntie Josie was just weird, but that actually they were quite funny together. Colly was definitely in a good mood and even Shanice seemed relaxed, particularly as the news coverage of the attempted 'cat-napping' (which is what the papers had called it) had increased the number of visitors to the park and for now at least the bills could be paid.

Kevin had managed to speak to most of the animals in the park and the conversation was all about who did what to stop the criminals. The only animals he hadn't spoken to were Fyodor and Fefina. He had tried, but even though Fyodor was now back in his enclosure recovering from his injuries, the leopards only seemed to be visible when the visitors were there, so he couldn't get any time to speak.

The amazing thing was Kevin had managed to talk to Albert and confessed he had told Mr. Collingwood about his secret. The animals have convened another special residents meeting and after the usual complaints and unhelpful comments from the hippos they had agreed that Kevin could translate for Mr. Collingwood in a special meeting, as a way to help the animals get what they needed. The orangutans had apparently been very excited at the prospect of a new water supply and tangle-free hair.

Everything seemed positive, the only exception being it was Kevin's last day before school started and he did not particularly want to go back to lessons, teachers and thick school gravy.

'Kevin!'

A dark voice behind him made him turn in surprise. It was Fyodor who had come to the edge of his enclosure, behind him about 5 metres away was Fefina, rolling on her back in the last warm rays of the day.

'Thank you, Kevin.'

'Oh, Fyodor, I'm glad you are OK.' Kevin dropped his voice to a whisper. 'How are you and Fefina getting on?'

'Well, apparently attacking that driver and trying to protect her was much better than bringing her rocks or blowing up my face.'

They both laughed.

'Kevin, I wanted you to be the first to know. Fefina is expecting cubs.'

As he spoke Fefina walked towards him and nuzzled her spotty neck against his, purring affectionately before flicking her tail and bounding back into the undergrowth, quickly pursued by her mate.

Kevin walked back towards the exit. There was a large, contented smile on his face. He felt strangely warm and snuggly inside. Harry was on the gate and Brutus bounded over to Kevin, his pink tongue lolling from side to side like he was trying to eat a gigantic worm.

'All right, boy, there's a good boy,' Kevin said, rubbing the little dog's tummy.

'Still talking to dumb animals then, huh?'

Shanice had appeared and was scowling in her usual way. Kevin was used to her by now and just smiled. For a fleeting moment he thought about Colly and Josie, Fyodor and Fefina, and considered asking Shanice out to the cinema.

'I, uh, well, I thought maybe if you...'

As he spoke he heard the familiar coo of the woodpigeon from the tree behind.

'You're so silly, so sooo silly.'

Maybe they were right. He shook the idea from his head.

'Nothing, it's OK. I guess I'll see you around.'

'Oh. Yes. Colly said he offered you a Saturday job, so I suppose I can't get rid of you that easily.'

'No, see ya, Shanice.'

'Kevin.'

'Yep?' He turned, expecting another put down.

'Do you want to go to the cinema some time?'

She was smiling. It wasn't a perfectly natural smile, but he could tell she was trying.

The Beginning.

Lightning Source UK Ltd.
Milton Keynes UK
UKHW021305140521
383721UK00007B/283